The Orphans of Mordecai's Castle

The Haven

By

Cara Simmons

God bless,
Cara Simmons
Eph 3:20

The Orphans of Mordecai's Castle
The Haven
by Cara Simmons

Printed in the United States of America

ISBN 978-1-60266-714-3

Unless otherwise indicated, Bible quotations are taken from
the Holy Bible, King James Version.

Front cover illustration by Julie Ball.

www.xulonpress.com

I would like to thank my Lord and Savior Jesus Christ Who has been a friend to me ever since He came into my heart when I was just a little girl. Thanks to all the children who willingly and eagerly listened to my stories, and to my Mom and Dad who raised me in a God-fearing home. Much love and thanks to Ryan, Nathan, Rebecca, Joanna, and Christa for putting up with me as their sister. Lastly, I want to thank my husband and children for all their support, prayers, ideas, and encouragement in the process of making this book. You are all a blessing to me. I love you.

God bless,
Cara

Chapter Index

Preface

L
ess than one-hundred-fifty years ago, most children had
two books for reading choices in their homes, *The Holy
Bible* and *The Pilgrim's Progress*. Children's fiction today
typically contains witchcraft, spiritualism, substance abuse,
immorality, rebellion, and an overall hatred of authority. The
reason why this wicked media has flourished is obvious; our
culture has rejected its Christian heritage. It was not that long
ago when Sundays were a day of rest for everyone. People
generally did their errands Monday through Saturday, and on
Sundays, stores remained closed with the majority of people
in church.

This book takes place at a time in our nation's history
when the effects of "The Great Awakening" revival were
waning. Where God once had a central place in the class-
rooms of our nation, other ideas began to emerge to take His
place. In the biology classes, the theory of evolution slowly
began to replace creationism. It was in these schoolrooms
that students were introduced to reading materials that began
to urge them away from biblical principles to a more "free
spirited" attitude. Fortunately, there was still a Biblical core
to our culture, and children were not bombarded by the
ungodliness in all forms of media as they are today. This

spiritual condition of our land makes it vitally important that we provide children with as much Biblically based material as possible to combat the negative messages they continually receive.

In many cases, the standards in Christian fiction written in our day have declined along with the standards in our society. Some would argue that standards must change because society no longer accepts those standards. We must remember, however, that our standard is the Bible. The Bible never changes, and the standards contained within it never change as well.

Many books compromise the message of the gospel to reach a broader audience, but this book keeps the gospel message at the forefront while telling a very compelling story. It is Cara's vision that this book would give both parents and children a choice in Godly reading material. It is her hope that you find this book inspirational as well as entertaining.

In Christ,

Joe Simmons

Meet The Characters:

Margie – fourteen years of age; petite, dark-haired mother-image for the orphans

Kia – four years old

Larissa – five years old

Teddy – seven years old; gentle, tender-hearted little boy

Brock – fifteen; as the oldest he takes responsibility for the little group

James Carver – the missionary who introduced the orphans to the saving power of Christ; he is sailing with them to Florida to find new homes

Blossom – three years old; the youngest orphan

Adam – a sailor on the *Haven*

Aaron – twelve; one of the young men Brock always takes with him as he explores.

Oakley – eight; best friends with Teddy

Mr. and Mrs. Talley – the caretakers of the orphans while they lived at the orphanage

Scotty – nine years old; has shocking red hair, spirited, and is always testing his elders

Mark – thirteen; a big help to Brock when it comes to exploring the grounds

Mordecai – the name etched on the door of the laboratory at the bottom floor of the castle

Tina – ten; she enjoys helping Margie with the younger children

Nettle – ten-year-old village girl, who earns the nickname **Nellie**

Jack (King Farrell) – the sailor who built the castle seventy-five years ago

Sadie – Nettle's mother and Bryan's sister; married to Raul

Buttercup – Nettle's aunt, who is married to Bryan; mother to Summer, Wheaton, and Tomas

Raul – Nettle's father; married to Sadie; one of the elders

Bryan – Nettle's uncle, married to Buttercup

Jared Bones – warrior who came looking for gold on the island

Matthew – leader of the villagers; Sadie and Bryan's father; married to Pearlie;

Kato – seventeen years old; newly married to Mariah

Mariah – Nettle's older sister, married to Kato

Hugh – married to Rosa

Rosa – married to Hugh – has no children

Pearlie – married to Matthew; is the village doctor and has knowledge of herbal medicine

Bruno – Captain of the *Jellyfish*

McAllister – first mate of the *Jellyfish*; Bruno's right hand man

Lily- Jack Farrell's wife; mother of Pearlie; once known as Queen Lily

Monty – one of the sailors on the *Jellyfish*

They that go down to the sea in ships, that do business in great waters; These see the works of the LORD, and his wonders in the deep. For he commandeth, and raiseth the stormy wind, which lifteth up the waves thereof. They mount up to the heaven, they go down again to the depths: their soul is melted because of trouble. They reel to and fro, and stagger like a drunken man, and are at their wits' end. Then they cry unto the LORD in their trouble, and he bringeth them out of their distresses. He maketh the storm a calm, so that the waves thereof are still. Then are they glad because they be quiet; so he bringeth them unto their desired haven.

Psalms 107:23-30

Prologue

The light was dim in the long hall, but it did nothing to hide the grey paint flaking off the old door. A faint light showed through the underside and peeked out along the uneven edges. A group of children huddled nearby as they listened to the loud voices coming from behind the thin, off-white walls. Their little faces showed apprehension and worry as they heard their beloved Mr. and Mrs. Talley arguing with the stranger.

"Please give us some more time!" Mr. Talley's voice pleaded. "My brother is coming from England with the money and then we will be able to pay you."

"This is not a trick to keep Talley's Orphanage, is it? You have proof that he is coming?" The deep voice of the stranger spoke. The sound sent shivers down the little ones' backs. The smallest child pushed closer to the oldest girl and hid her face in her dress.

There was a rustle of paper and then Mr. Talley replied, "Here is the telegram that arrived yesterday. He will be coming in on the steamship tomorrow afternoon."

A chair scraped inside the room. The children scampered away quickly as his voice neared the door. "Then I will be waiting for you at the harbor tomorrow afternoon. Good day to you." The door creaked opened and out walked a tall, gangly man. He paused as he shrugged into his coat and put on his hat. A sneeze brought his head up and he frowned at the small faces he saw peering at him from the doorways of the large entry hall where he stood. "Bah," he mumbled, his bushy eyebrows touching in the middle. "This place will soon be mine and all those pesky rats will be eliminated. Children don't make money, but a hotel certainly would!" He sneered at the children and slipped out the front door.

"Is he gone?" whispered a little voice from behind one of the doorways.

"Yes, I think he is," answered the oldest girl named Margie. "It is safe to come out now." She smiled at the children and reached out to the touch the long braid of the girl beside her. "Don't worry, everything will be just fine."

Brock, the oldest of the orphans, stepped forward and cleared his throat. "I have an idea! I know it will not be much, but if we collect all the money we have and give it to Mr. Talley, maybe it will hold the stranger off for a while."

Heads quickly nodded in agreement and children scampered off to their sleeping quarters, the girls on one side of the large house and the boys on the other. Five minutes later they all regrouped in the hall and Brock counted up the handful of coins. Like he said it was not much, but they still had to try.

Once again the children all gathered in front of the big, grey door. They waited quietly for the door to open again, knowing full well they were not allowed inside the office. Inside that room sat all the files to each child, stating the reason why each one had been brought to the orphanage. None of the children really cared about going inside anyway because the room always brought back painful memories of the first day each one had arrived.

The door slowly opened. Jolly Mr. Talley, who had been the father figure to them, suddenly looked old and tired. He held the door open for his wife and closed it behind them. Together they looked at the group of young ones standing before them. "My dear children," smiled Mrs. Talley, "why are you all looking so glum? Cheer up, my pets, for all will be well!"

Brock approached Mr. Talley and took his wrinkled hand. He poured the coins into it, closed Mr. Talley's fist over them, and stepped back. Tears came to Mr. Talley's eyes as he realized what the children were doing. He also knew that refusing the gift would be rejection to his little tribe. He looked up at his wife and winked at her. "You sure did a right fine job of teaching your children about selflessness."

With tears in her eyes, Mrs. Talley shook her head. "You silly man, it hasn't been just me teaching them. Why, these children…" A loud knock on the door interrupted her. She walked towards the door and opened it to find a young man standing on the step with a frightened little boy in his arms. Both of them had shockingly bright red hair and fair skin.

The man shifted from one foot to the other and looked around nervously. "I have here a little orphan boy," he stated. "His name is Scotty. His mother died a few weeks ago and there is no one who can care for him."

Mrs. Talley looked from the man to the little boy. "What relation are you to the lad? He resembles you quite a bit."

The red haired man's eyes flashed for an instant, but the look disappeared as fast as it had come. He sighed. "I am his father." He quickly added, "But like I said, his mother died a few weeks back and I cannot care for him. I am going to look for work. There should be some work for me in the harbor. When I get established and can care for the boy, I will return for him." He pulled the little boy's arms away from his neck and handed him to Mrs. Talley.

"Won't you come inside, Mister…?"

The man took a step backwards down the concrete stairs. "The surname is McAllister and no, I don't want to come in."

"But I need you to sign the form of release for us to care for Scotty."

"No. I do not want to sign anything. My word is all you need. Good day to you."

Without another word he turned around, away from the sight of his young son reaching out his little arms to him. "Dada!" Scotty cried as he watched his father walk away and disappear down the busy streets of the city.

Margie's eyes filled with tears as the scene unfolded before her. A pain began in the pit of her stomach and moved slowly up until it lodged in her throat. It had been different for her when her parents had passed away, but this toddler would forever have the image burned in his tender heart of a father who did not care and had abandoned him. She knew he would need a lot of love and special attention over the next few years. In her heart she silently made a promise to help watch over the poor, hurting boy.

CHAPTER ONE

Shipwrecked!

The ship rocked back and forth, as the giant waves crashed against the sides of the small vessel. The storm had relentlessly tossed the ship around for five long hours, as if it was a small toy. Down inside the belly of the ship, a group of children lay huddled on their thin mattresses trying to sleep. There were eleven children in all. The girls were on one side, and the boys on the other, separated by a faded blue muslin curtain.

Margie, the oldest girl of the bunch, sat up to listen. Straining her ears against the noise of the storm, she faintly heard the sound of sniffling.

"Larissa, is that you?" she whispered softly into the darkness. Being the motherly type, Margie got up from her hay-stuffed mattress and began to make her way across the wooden floor. The sniffling continued, and with it, a little whimper. "Blossom? Are you okay?" Suddenly a big wave rocked the ship, and Margie fell over onto the sleeping girls.

"Ouch! Who is that? Margie? What did you go and do that for?" a little voice squeaked out from underneath her.

Margie quickly got up and knelt down by the mattress so she would not be thrown off balance again.

"I am sorry, Kia. A big wave knocked me down! Did I hurt you much?"

Four-year old Kia shook her head as she rolled over onto her back. Margie adjusted the thin blanket and kissed her forehead. "There now, is that better?" Margie leaned over and whispered in Kia's ear, "Thank you for catching me so I wouldn't get hurt." She patted the girl's cheek and continued toward the sound of whimpering, this time crawling so she would not lose her balance again. Little hands reached out to touch her as she passed the girls' beds, and Margie always responded with a gentle hug.

She arrived at Larissa's bed and whispered, "Are you okay, Lissa?" The little girl's back was to her. She touched Larissa's hair. "Turn over, Honey, and tell me what's wrong."

Larissa rolled over and looked up into Margie's face. She had great big tears streaming down her cheeks. "I'm s-scared of the big waves! It might knock the b-boat over!" She covered her face with her hands and sobbed loudly. Margie sat down next to Larissa and pulled her onto her lap.

"Now don't you worry, Lissa." Margie comforted her as she stroked her long, dark hair. "Many boats have made it through rougher seas then this. Let me tell you a story about when Jesus and His disciples were caught in a storm." Suddenly, four little girls all sat up in their beds. They wanted to hear the story too!

A light tapping caught her attention, and she looked over towards the curtain. A little face was peering around the side inquisitively. A little voice piped up, "Can I come and listen too, Margie?"

Margie could not help but smile at the boy. Teddy was the most gentle, loving little boy she had ever known. He was very curious as all children are, but he never repeated an offence, and always took correction with a humble attitude. He dearly loved the Lord and had his heart fixed on serving Him in everything.

"Of course you can, Teddy. Come and sit down on this side of the curtain." As Teddy entered the girls' side, he was not alone. A trail of five other boys followed behind him.

Brock, the oldest of the group, was the last to enter carrying a lantern in his hand. He grinned sheepishly at Margie as he sat down and carefully set the lantern down next to him. "They couldn't sleep in this storm. I did all I could to help, but they were just too scared. The minute they heard you say 'story' there was nothing I could do to stop them from getting up."

The soft glow of the light lit up the small area and Margie smiled tenderly at all the children. These children were very dear to her and she loved every one of them. They all had lots in common, the main thing being that they were orphans. They had all lost their parents in different tragedies, but they also had gained a new Father when a missionary had come and taught them about Jesus. James Carver had come to their orphanage in Boston a year ago and spent a couple of weeks telling them about God's love. His message had been new to them, and they had been doubtful about it at first. After all, they had been through great heartache, and it had been hard to accept the fact that Jesus loved them enough to die for their sins and rise again. Teddy had been the first to accept the Lord into his heart, and it was through his gentle words and living testimony that won many of the others to Christ.

Margie settled down with baby Blossom on her lap and began, "It had been a long day of preaching for Jesus and His disciples and they were very tired. It was night when they all climbed into a boat and set sail for the other side. During their ride, Jesus took a little pillow and fell asleep in the corner of their boat. While He was sleeping, a storm came up and started shaking the boat like a little toy."

"Like ours is doing now?" Oakley, a little eight-year-old boy, with freckles and curly hair, asked.

"Yes, Oakley, like ours, though it might have been a lot stronger. Jesus' disciples grew very scared and thought they were going to sink. They shouted to Jesus, "Wake up, Master! Help us with this storm! We are all going to die!" Jesus slowly got up and looked around at the storm. Then He raised His arms and said to the wind, "Peace be still!" Immediately the wind stopped blowing. The waves quieted down, and it was as if there had never been a storm. His disciples were amazed at the power of Jesus. Even the winds and the sea obeyed His voice. So you see, children, we do not need to be afraid because He is here with us, and we can have peace like He had even in the midst of this storm."

Outside, the storm raged on, the waves growing bigger as the wind tossed the ship around the open sea. One huge wave bore down on the battered ship and violently crashed into the side. All the children screamed in terror. The lantern slid away from Brock, wobbled back and forth and toppled over. Brock quickly reached out to grab the handle, but pulled his hand back when he saw the hot flame shoot out and hungrily lick up the spilled oil. The tongue of fire grabbed at a blanket hanging over the edge of one of the mattresses, quickly spreading over the bed. Larissa stood up and began screaming for help, as the fire grew closer to her.

"Brock, get Lissa!" Margie shouted as she leaped up with baby Blossom in her arms. "Quickly, children, there isn't time to take anything! Get out of here as fast as you can! Hurry!"

Brock rushed to Larissa's side and pulled her to safety just as the fire reached the spot where she had been standing. He pulled her out of harms way and began to beat at the flames with another tattered blanket, but the wood inside the ship was very dry, and the flame spread rapidly. The room quickly filled with thick, choking smoke, and he could hear the children coughing as they breathed it in. As the heat of the fire grew more intense, he knew it was essential to get all the children out. He looked around for one of the older boys.

"Mark! Run and get Mr. Carver!"

Without hesitation, the thirteen-year-old raced ahead of the children lining up near the ladder and ran up to the deck. Margie and Brock quickly herded the frightened group toward safety. Some were crying softly, and as each passed Margie, she gently reminded them, "Trust in Jesus. He won't leave us."

Brock climbed the ladder first and helped guide the children out onto the wet deck. He found a long piece of rope and tied it to the large spar that held the biggest sail of the ship. "Hold tight to that rope and don't let go!" he hollered above the wind. As the children came out of the hold, they grabbed onto the rope and held on for dear life. The wind whistled eerily and the waves splashed loudly around them.

Mark appeared from nowhere and hollered above the wind, "He's coming!" Brock shielded his eyes from the driving rain and was relieved to see the strong form of James Carver rushing toward them.

"What happened?" he asked Brock, grabbing little Kia as she reached the top of the steps. More sailors joined the group, and they hurried down into the hold to try to put out the fire.

"The lantern fell when one of the waves hit the ship! I'm so sorry! I should not have even lit it in a storm like this."

"Don't feel badly, son. It wasn't your fault. You just get all the children into the lifeboat while we put out the fire."

Brock looked into his mentor's eyes. There was an anxiousness hidden there and Brock could see that Mr. Carver's reasoning went much deeper then what he was saying. There was a chance they might not be able to put out the fire, but Mr. Carver was concerned for the children's safety and future. Brock put his fears aside, and with Margie and some of the sailor's help, they pulled the tarp off the lifeboat and had all the little ones climb inside. When all eleven were safely in, Brock took Mr. Carver's arm.

"You are coming with us aren't you? You need to be safe too."

James looked at the young man and said, "I am burdened for the sailors on this ship, Brock. Many of them are still lost in their sin and I fear for their lives. What if this is the only opportunity they will get to hear about the Lord? If we can't put this fire out, then I want to make sure they have a chance to hear the Gospel one more time."

Brock choked back a sob. He understood, but inside he felt a little selfish. "We need you too, sir. What if something happens to us while we are in the lifeboat?"

"We all need to rely on the Lord in every situation. We don't always know the reason for things, but we do know we are in the Lord's hands. Trust in Him and do not fear. He is our Haven, and He will never leave you without a refuge." Mr. Carver reached into his coat pocket and pulled out a little, black Bible. "Here, take this with you. You can read to the little ones from the Psalms. It will put their minds at rest. Now go, Brock, and watch over His little flock."

Brock nodded bravely as the sailors lowered the boat over the side. A sailor named Adam, who was standing near the rail, leaned over and handed a pail and knife to Brock.

"We will keep the rope secured to the back of the boat so you don't drift away. If anything should happen to the ship and we can't put the fire out, cut the rope. There is a two-day supply of water and food under the seats. Be wise and use it sparingly. There are a lot of you." He looked down at Brock. "God go with you."

All the children hunkered down in the small boat as the *Haven* drifted away from them. The rain was still coming down so Brock and Margie took the tarp from the side and pulled it over everyone to help keep them somewhat dry. They tucked it into the sides, around the older children on the outside edges of the lifeboat, and put the littlest ones in the middle. There they rested inside the rocking lifeboat, sheltered under the green tarp, listening to Brock read from the book of Psalms.

It seemed like hours before the storm finally grew calmer and the frightened children relaxed as the waves outside the boat gradually ceased. They did not have to be frightened anymore of a big wave overturning their boat into the sea. Brock waited to hear the call of one of the sailors for the okay to come back on the *Haven*. "Please, Lord, help me hear it soon. I want to be back safely on the ship." All was quiet outside. Brock decided to peek out from under the tarp and see if the sailors had put out the fire. He looked out and breathed in the clear, crisp air. The water was peaceful and the clouds were opening up to reveal a full moon. He glanced behind him toward the stern of the big ship and gasped.

Margie had felt the tarp shift and noticed that Brock had pulled it down. She cautiously poked her head out and closed her eyes as the fresh air hit her face. She overheard Brock's gasp and quickly turned in his direction.

"What's wrong?" she asked, as a deep fear gripped her stomach, and then she saw it. By the light of the moon, she could see him holding up a broken piece of rope.

Panic threatened to overtake her as she frantically scanned the horizon for anything that resembled a ship. She looked at Brock. "What are we going to do?"

Sensing the fear in her voice, Brock knew he had to remain calm for her and for all the other children, who had started to pop up from beneath the tarp.

"Is the storm over?" Scotty asked.

"Can we go back to the boat now? I feel so cramped!" Oakley complained as he tried to straighten out his legs.

"Ouch! Cut that out, Oaks," yelled Aaron. "You're kicking me!"

"That's enough boys," Brock sternly scolded them. "I know we are all uncomfortable in this small boat, but we need to try to make the best of our situation." He tucked the bit of rope behind him. He hoped to keep the children from finding out about the ship as long as he could. He scanned the lifeboat and grimaced at how cramped the children already looked.

"Okay everyone! Listen up! Before anything else happens here, we need to make some rules. First off, nobody is to stand up on this boat. It is already very tipsy, and we do not need someone knocking us all out. Secondly..."

"Bro-o-ck?" a voice quivered from the middle.

"What is it, Tina?"

"Where is the *Haven*? I can't see it anywhere!"

Brock prayed for the right words. He did not want to strike fear in the hearts of these little ones left in his care.

"The rope broke during the storm, and we drifted away from the ship." He quickly continued when he saw the glittering of tears in the eyes of the children. "But do not worry! Before we left, Adam told me there was some food and water stored underneath the seats of the boat. I am sure Mr. Carver will come looking for us when it is daylight and we will be fine. The Lord will not abandon us, and He will get us to safety, just like Paul and all the prisoners on the ship in Acts. Remember how the angel appeared to Paul during that big storm? He told them they would all survive and they did."

"Did an angel appear to you?" Oakley questioned Brock.

"Well, no, but the Lord promises He will never leave us nor forsake us."

"What if the boat sinks and we all drown?" Oakley looked uncertainly at Brock.

"Do not think about the 'what-ifs'". Mr. Carver will rescue us before that happens."

"But what if he can't find us?" Oakley was persistent.

Ignoring the comment, Brock said, "Let us pray for our safety. The Lord is in the midst of wherever two or more are gathered. How many are in our group?"

"Eleven." Teddy spoke up. "That means the Lord is in the midst of us five times over!"

Margie smiled. "That's right. So we have nothing to fear now, do we?" As Margie bowed her head while Brock prayed, she silently added her own prayer for strength and wisdom to help with all the children's questions and fears.

When they were through praying, a wonderful sense of peace filled their hearts. The sunrise that morning set the sky aglow with pink and orange, and even though their future seemed dim, they were reassured of God's loving care over them, and rested under the shadow of His wings.

as close to each other as brother and sister. As children came and went from the orphanage, Margie and Brock remained. The children that stayed grew to look up to Margie and Brock. Margie was the tenderhearted sister they all needed, and Brock was the gentle, levelheaded older brother. Mr. and Mrs. Talley had done a good job providing for the children, but their hands were full with all they had to do and that did not leave much time for cuddling and comforting the children. Margie had seen to it to fill that void and all the children loved her dearly.

Brock's thoughts shifted to their present situation. "It's my fault we are in this mess! If only I had been more careful with that lantern! If only I had held onto it instead of being dumb enough to set it on the floor!" He squeezed his eyes shut in frustration and clenched his fists. How he wished this nightmare would end! He longed to see the *Haven* sail up and rescue them all from this frightful situation. Even though he was fifteen, he felt very young and immature to be responsible for all these children. He yearned to be back under the guidance of James Carver, to be able to ask him for advice.

"Brock?" A gentle voice to his right snapped him back to reality. He glanced towards Teddy, who was looking at him with a question in his eyes. "Are you okay?"

Brock's clenched fist, which had been resting on the boy's shoulder, was twitching, and he could see Teddy was concerned. He relaxed, opened, and closed his hands a few times, then smiled. "Sure, Teddy, I'm just a little tense, that's all." He patted Teddy's shoulder encouragingly, and silently breathed a quick prayer of thanks to the Lord for pulling him out of the pit of despair. He knew it would not be the last time, but he had the Lord on his side.

"I'm thirsty!" a voice complained to his left.

"Yeah, me too!" Another child picked up the chant and soon everyone was whining about how they all felt like they were going to die. Brock felt like Moses when the Israelites were complaining for water. He looked at Margie, who was waiting for his direction.

"Okay, Margie. Let's pull out some food and water for them all. It's almost ten o'clock anyway."

Margie turned as best she could in the cramped area she was in and pulled out a carton from under the seat. Inside were rations of soda crackers, dried meat, and water for three people for two days. There was one more box under her seat, and two more near Brock. Brock tried to follow the instructions on each carton, but he felt he needed to save some extra just in case they were out to sea longer then two days, God forbid!

The children eagerly reached out for the precious food and water, and after a quick prayer of thanks for their scant meal, they ate the crackers and dried beef slowly, savoring each bite, hoping this would be the last time they would eat aboard the tiny boat.

Scotty, who was nine years old and had a head of bright red hair, finished his snack, and looked enviously at all the other children still eating. His belly still rumbled in hunger, and he groaned as the sweat poured down his face. The sun was directly overhead now, and there was not a cloud in the sky to shield them from its intense heat. Scotty leaned over the edge of the boat and touched the cool, sparkling water. Oh, how he wanted to jump in and cool off! Maybe Brock would let him if he asked him nicely. He looked up to find Brock studying him, almost as if Brock knew what he was thinking.

"Don't even think about it, Scotty. If you got out the whole boat would rock and flip us all overboard. We can't risk doing that or else we might lose all our food and water, not to mention those who can't swim!"

Scotty groaned again. "But I'm so hot! My face feels hot and tight, and my eyes hurt! You said Mr. Carver would rescue us today! Why hasn't he found us yet?"

Brock could sense this was leading to trouble. Scotty was the one who always acted out in anger, and he had a temper unlike anybody else. He had to tread lightly with the boy or else he feared that Scotty might throw *him* overboard. He held his hand up for silence. "Scotty, I know what I said, but I don't know what is going to happen. I do know the Lord is in control of this situation, and He is going to take care of us. Mr. Carver may not be the one to rescues us; God may send someone else along. Or else we might find land or something, but however the Lord chooses to save us, we will go along with His will. God knows best and I trust Him. He is our Father, and He will take care of us."

"Yeah, like my real father, who just left me at the orphanage? Fathers don't care. How do I know God cares about me?" Scotty slouched down in the boat and turned angrily away from Brock.

"Dear God," Brock prayed silently, "break through that boy's hurting heart. Only You can show Him how much You love him."

"We should put the tarp over the children so they won't get sunstroke." Margie said, pointing to some of the children who were sleeping. Without a word, Brock leaned forward, took the edge of the tarp, and pulled it over the group, Margie pulling the other side. It would get hot and stuffy underneath, but it was better then getting sick from the sun beating down on them. Would this day ever end?

Nighttime finally arrived and with it came relief from the heat and a moonless sky. A slight wind steadily pushed them on, an unseen finger guiding their little boat to a special place already picked out for them. They all slept fitfully, snuggled together as close to each other as they could so they would stay warm as the night air grew cooler. They were all thankful for the tarp that helped in keeping some of the heat in. All night long as they slept, their boat sailed through the rippling waves. It seemed to have a destination in mind and did not veer to the left or the right.

It was morning when Brock opened his eyes and stuck his head outside the tarp. He looked around, dreading another long day in the cramped boat, when his eyes spied a clump of trees off in the distance. He strained harder, hoping to get a clearer picture before he announced the news to the children.

"Hey, everyone, I see land ahead!"

Ten heads all popped up quickly, pushing back the tarp in excitement.

"Where is it?"

"Are we still in America?"

"Will Mr. Carver be there?"

Brock smiled at all the questions, "I don't know where it is, but I know it will feel good to stretch my legs again!" With hope restored from the sighting of land, all eleven children eagerly looked out towards the horizon wishing their boat would go faster.

It was a couple of hours before they floated close enough to land so Brock could get out and pull them the rest of the way. With the help of Mark and Aaron, they were able to pull it up onto the beach. All the children leaped out and ran around the sand shouting for sheer joy. They had been very patient during the whole situation, but it felt wonderful to be able to run around on solid ground again.

Brock took the older boys with him to explore the outskirts of the beach, and Margie remained with the other children. She joined in their game of tag, just so she could get the kinks out of her legs. After running around for fifteen minutes, she sat down next to Blossom and Kia who were playing in the sand. "What are you making?" she asked.

Kia answered, "We're makin' a castle!"

"Oh, what a beautiful castle, Kia!" Margie commented, "Who lives there?"

"The king and queen, of course." Kia grabbed a clump of wet dirt and used both hands to form a wall. "I like castles. I wish I could live in one someday."

Margie smiled. "Castles are very neat. They are full of mysteries, trap doors, tunnels, and hidden spaces. I have never been in one, but I would like to go in one too."

Kia stopped. "Could you help me build one? Mine keeps falling down."

"Sure! Let me get some more water to make the sand stick better." Immersed in the building of their sandcastle, she barely heard Brock's shout of excitement.

"Margie!"

She looked up to see Brock come running breathlessly out of the woods.

"There's an overgrown trail leading up into the rocks of the mountain. We started to go up, but I did not want to go too far. Maybe there is a village there and we can find some help."

"Is it safe Brock?" Margie was worried about all the stories she had heard about cannibals.

"I believe the Lord brought us to this place for a reason, and I believe He will keep us safe from anything harmful. Come on! Get the children together, and we will soon find out what is up there."

The children were excited to go exploring, so they grouped together behind Brock, with Margie in the back with the younger ones. They followed the trail overgrown with years of growth which led through the woods and up into the cliffs. There was excitement in the air, at the unknowns that lay around each corner. Margie watched, as the group in front of her gradually grew further away while she remained with the slower children. They went around a corner and disappeared from her view. It grew very quiet, and she strained her ears for any noise of the children. Where had they gone? A few birds chirped and an insect sang in the brush, but there were no voices of the other children talking. Glancing around the forest, she saw many different fruit trees, full of ripe, juicy looking fruit. Her mouth watered and she considered going off the trail to pick some, but a shout stopped her in her tracks. Brock was running towards her, with Aaron and Mark hot on his heels. Brock stopped in front of her and said, "You won't believe what we saw!"

"What? What did you see?"

"Can I tell her Brock? I saw it first!" Mark pleaded with Brock for permission.

"Well someone better tell me or else I will go find out for myself!" Margie figured it must be something extraordinary by the way they were so excited to tell her.

"Up on the hill…" Brock said.

"…there's a castle!" Mark quickly added before Brock could continue.

"A what?" gasped Margie?

"A castle!" Aaron put in quickly.

By this time, all the other children had caught up with them, and they were all speaking at once. Jumping around in excitement, it was all Margie and Brock could do to get them to be quiet. Finally, Brock whistled through his fingers, and they quickly quieted down.

"Now listen everyone, I know we've seen a neat castle, but we don't know if anyone lives there or not. If it is abandoned, it might have some spots that are not safe. The floors and bridge may be rotten. I don't want anybody getting hurt or doing anything foolish. You will all follow behind me. I am responsible for all of you now, and you must obey me until Mr. Carver finds us. I am the leader in this group now, and you must all listen to Margie and me. Understand?"

Everyone nodded in agreement and said, "Yes, sir."

"Good. Now everyone line up, and let's all go together!"

The group hiked up the steep path with Brock in the lead and Margie bringing up the rear. All the children were breathless with excitement: a real castle! What wondrous things would they find? Did anyone live there? Who had built it? With many unspoken questions on their minds, the children trekked up the last bit of hill. When they reached the top, they found themselves looking over a large meadow filled with straight rows of fruit trees. Old, split rail fences, that were rotting and falling down now, surrounded areas that once may have been gardens. The trail continued a little further and stopped at the edge of a large drawbridge that stretched across a large gap of about fifty feet between two cliffs. About a hundred feet down they could see the water lapping at the sides of the rock walls, which had been made smooth by the process.

Brock thought he saw a trail along the bottom edge of the opposite cliff, and mentally stored the idea to explore it in the future. He stopped at the foot of the bridge and everyone stopped behind him.

"I will go first to make sure it is safe." Brock carefully moved across the boards, checking any spots that may have become rotten. When he got to the other side, he motioned them over and said, "One at a time! Stay in the middle! It will be fine. Come on over, everyone!"

With that, the orphans slowly went across the bridge, and entered a new world of wonder and excitement with all the unknowns that lay beyond those old walls of the castle.

CHAPTER THREE

Mordecai's Castle

The old, wooden bridge seemed to sway as Mark slowly made his way to the other side. The children in front of him stepped cautiously over the dark gray boards that creaked beneath their feet. Looking to the left, he saw a massive cliff on either side of a great canal, with dark, choppy waters lapping at the bottom of the rocks. There was an even larger mountain towering behind the castle, like an enormous giant standing guard over his fortress. The rock face went straight down, as if a knife had cut it right in half. It all seemed like something he had read in a book, and it hardly seemed possible that this was really happening. Maybe there were even medieval knights behind the gate of the castle, watching from inside their shiny armor!

"Mark!" He heard Aaron calling from behind.

He turned slightly and answered, "What is it, Aaron?"

"Isn't this neat? Seems like something you would read about in a book!"

"That's just what I was thinking!" Mark laughed as they reached the other side. "I can't wait to see what is beyond that gate! Maybe Brock will let us go exploring with him!"

Aaron grinned excitedly. "Yeah, I wonder if we will find treasure inside! Wouldn't it be great to have some money to give to Mr. Carver when he comes looking for us? Then he wouldn't have to worry about how he would feed us all, and we could help more orphans!"

Mark chuckled. Leave it to Aaron to think of others before thinking of himself. Mark had to agree though it would be neat to find some buried treasure.

The children made it across safely, and found themselves in front of the tall gate that blocked them from getting inside the stone castle. Brock was not sure how they were going to get beyond the gate sealed tight between the two walls. The weight of the door had left a deep rut in the mud around the edges, and there was no way they could budge it. Brock instructed Margie to line the children up along the wall away from the edge of the cliffs where it would be safer. When everyone sat with their backs to the cold, stone wall, he called Mark and Aaron. Together they went off to explore the walls of the castle. Brock was hoping he could find another entrance inside the castle before nightfall, so they could all take refuge inside. It would be the perfect place to stay until Mr. Carver returned and rescued them.

Green ivy covered the entire wall of the east side, making it hard to spot any windows to where they could climb. There was a tower on either end of the wall, and another smaller one exactly in the middle. Brock pointed out the lookout spot where the guards must have once stood, looking out over the long canals, watching for danger. "There must be a wonderful view from up there," he commented, "I can't wait to go up and look sometime!"

Brock calculated that there were about three floors inside, not including the towers along the roof or a possible dungeon underneath.

The side of the wall stretched on a long way, but finally they reached the corner and turned along the backside of the castle. The sheer cliff of the mountain stood about fifty feet away from them and the wall.

Mark almost fell over trying to look up at the top of the mountain from where he stood on the ground. Aaron laughed and playfully socked him in the shoulder.

"My father would have loved to climb that rock!" whispered Mark. Aaron's playfulness suddenly disappeared, and he quickly gave Mark's shoulder a reassuring squeeze. He understood Mark's fascination with the mountain: Mark's father had loved the outdoors, but it had been his undoing. He had taken a plunge from halfway up on one of his climbs in the White Mountains of New Hampshire when Mark had been just a toddler. His mother died of a lonely heart shortly after, and Mark had lived at the orphanage ever since.

Noticing that Brock was getting away from them, Mark quickly ran ahead with Aaron right on his heels.

It was while they were looking along the third wall that a strange bush caught Brock's attention, and he went closer to examine it. Seeing a pile of rocks hidden by the brush along the back touching the wall, he reached in and pushed a few to the side. A couple of small stones rolled away, revealing a hole underneath!

"Come on guys! Help me move these large rocks! This may be a secret passage leading to the inside!" They all struggled to move the crumbling debris away and discovered some stairs leading down into the darkness. It was cool and musty smelling. Brock went first and disappeared into the blackness.

"You guys coming?" His voice echoed in the tunnel.

"Don't you think we need a light? How are we going to find our way to the other side! This place is huge!" Aaron looked fearfully at Mark.

Mark shrugged. "I'm not going to miss this for the world!" He quickly followed Brock into the shadows.

Aaron stood alone outside, unsure of what he should do. He had no desire to get lost inside the pitch-black tunnel, and since he was the oldest *man* left to make decisions, he decided he would do the job of checking on the little ones. "I'm going to help Margie! I'll meet you out front!"

He barely heard Brock's answer as he ran around the last corner and found the children huddled together against the mossy stonewall.

Margie looked up in surprise. "Aaron? What happened? Where are the others?"

"They found a tunnel under the wall and are going to try to find a way through."

"You didn't want to go?" Margie smiled, but she knew Aaron had a soft heart. He pushed his toe around in the dirt. When he did not say anything, she knew he was embarrassed.

"That's okay. I could use your help in keeping the boys out of mischief. Maybe you could sit with them and tell them what you saw while you were exploring."

Aaron smiled gratefully at Margie for not making him look like a coward, and quickly went to sit with the boys. He soon had their attention while he told them of the tall towers along the walls, and of the mysterious hole leading down into the ground.

Margie watched the littlest ones slowly relax as the excitement of the day finally began to take its toll on them. One after the other they started to lean on the child next to them and fall asleep. Margie looked across the drawbridge at the landscape in front of them. It was beautiful and quiet, with a slight breeze blowing through the trees. The path they had traveled along to reach the castle had followed the base of the mountain; tall trees and flowering bushes hid it from her view from where she sat. With the castle nestled down in the nook between the two giants, Margie wondered if it was visible to any travelers on the ocean. The fear of never leaving the island caused panic to well up inside of Margie, but before it overcame her, she quietly bowed her head and prayed for someone to come and rescue them, and for the boys who were somewhere deep inside the castle. "Keep your hands on them every step of the way, dear Lord," she prayed. "I don't know what I would do if I didn't have them to help me!"

* * * * * * * * *

Brock and Mark slowly traveled down the narrow tunnel, the dirt floor feeling cool and hard under their bare feet. They felt their way along the cold, stone tunnel, and as they did, something odd began to happen: an eerie greenish-blue light began to glow as their hands touched certain rocks placed carefully along the sides. One rock after the other started to glow from their touch, lighting their way down the dry, musty-smelling path. Brock was delighted with this discovery. "Luminescent rocks! That is the neatest thing!" he said in wonder.

"Luma-nesin what? What does that mean?" Mark asked bewildered.

Brock smiled. "Lu-min-e-scent," he said slowly. "It simply means to glow. The rocks do not need heat to emit their light. It occurs through a chemical process activated by touch. Whoever made this castle sure knew how to use the wonders of God's creation! I wonder what else we will discover down here!"

Mark was thrilled to the bone too! He had always wanted to do something exciting like this! The path seemed endless, going deeper and farther down into the depths of the earth. He stopped and paused with Brock as he studied the rocks. Brock's face looked distorted in the peculiar, greenish light. Turning back towards the path, Mark noted the sound of water bubbling.

"Listen, Brock! Do you hear that?"

Brock paused and listened. "Yes, it sounds like a stream or something." He began walking again. "We're getting closer." He broke out running, eager to see where the sound was coming from. As they turned a corner, the glowing light became brighter, and the walls had green ripples from the reflection from some hidden river. Walking another fifty feet, they finally came out into a large cavern, where the river was flowing in front of them. The water had different sized glowing rocks in it, and some were poking out of the water, like stepping-stones leading all the way to the other side. Across the river, they could see some stairs carved into the sides of the walls leading up and disappearing around a corner. A large pond fed by the river was to their left, and there were hundreds of little glowing dots swimming around inside it. Brock went over and studied it closer.

"What is it?" Mark asked as he approached the water.

Science had always been Brock's favorite subject in school, and he racked his brain on what it could be that was streaking through the water. "I'm not sure yet, but I am going to find out." He walked over to the moss-covered stepping-stones, and glanced around for Mark, who was kneeling next to the water. "I'm going across!" he called.

Mark scrambled up and followed him across to the other side. Brock walked around looking at everything, not wanting to miss a thing. Underneath the stairs, he discovered a large wooden door with a rotting sign and faded words that read,

Mordecai's Lab

Brock rattled the knob of a door as Mark crowded close to him. "It's unlocked!" Upon Brock's gentle push, the door squeaked opened. Brock went in and Mark heard a thud.

"Ouch! I just ran into something!" Suddenly the same eerie green and blue light, activated by Brock's bump, lit up and filled the room. A table stood before them, covered with papers, rocks, and jars of glowing matter. Shelves lined the walls from floor to ceiling filled with rows of jars, containing mysterious formulas. Broken vials and more papers lay scattered around the floor.

Brock could feel the excitement welling up inside him. How he would love to stay and study everything in here, but he knew there were more important matters to deal with right now. "We will have more time to check things out later, but right now the others are still waiting for us. I am positive the stairs will lead us up, and we will be able to open the gate for Margie and the children. I am sure they are worried about us by now."

"I wonder who Mordecai was." Mark said as they shut the door to the lab. "Do you think this was his castle?"

"Maybe," Brock agreed, "but whoever he was, the lab obviously belonged to him. Maybe he was the king's personal inventor or something. Let's hurry up those stairs and see if they lead to the gate outside. We mustn't keep the others waiting any longer."

A little while later, they finally reached a large courtyard overgrown with grass and weeds. A large tree grew in the middle of the yard, and there were stairs on either side of the walls leading up to the ledge where the towers were. Across the yard in front of them was the gate, which had long chains connected to the top, and then led down to a large wheel with a crank on the side. Brock ran up to the door and pounded on it. "Margie! Can you hear me?"

A muffled voice came through the wood. "Brock, where have you been? I have been so worried!"

"I'll explain later! Get all the children away from the door! We're going to open it up!"

Brock counted to twenty before he took the long handle of the wheel and began cranking it. It was old and tarnished, and complained loudly as he turned it. "Mark! I need your help!" Mark stopped his exploring and ran over to assist Brock. Ever so slowly, the door began to rise up with grass and dirt hanging from the bottom. It left a long, deep rut of mud in the ground from where it had sat for so many years. When it was open enough for everyone to walk through without hitting their heads, Brock stopped cranking and secured the heavy, brass chain around the wheel; the door stayed where it was, and he whistled a shrill signal for all to enter.

The children ran into the courtyard and raced around screeching in excitement. Brock turned towards Margie. She seemed tired and worn out. "How are you doing?"

She avoided his question and said, "They seem very happy to have some place to run around." She turned away from him and looked at the children playing happily in the tall grass. Truth was she had thought something had happened to him, and had let fear overcome her. She had been so relieved to hear his voice from behind the door that it took every ounce of strength to keep from crying. The events of the last few days had slowly worn her down, and she wished for some time alone so she could cry and let it all out. She saw Kia trip and disappear into the tall grass. Her loud cry echoed through the courtyard. "I better go and kiss her boo-boo. You'll have to tell me about your adventure later, Brock."

Brock was puzzled as he watched Margie run over to Kia and reach down to pick her up. They had always been such good friends, and had been able to talk freely, ever since they had first known each other. They were like brother and sister! "Must be a girl thing," he brushed the thought away as he called the group back to him. When they were all gathered around him he said, "We never thanked the Lord for getting us safely to shore. We must all stop what we are doing and thank Him for His protection, and for guiding us safely inside this castle. It will be our shelter until Mr. Carver comes and rescues us."

As Mark bowed his head and closed his eyes, he secretly added his own prayer that they would have time to look around some more before someone rescued them from this intriguing place.

CHAPTER FOUR

The Deafening Howl

Teddy looked around for his friend Oakley, and found him playing tag with a couple of the other children. He ran up to Oakley and called to him, "Oaks, want to go exploring with me?"

Oakley paused for a moment, and Scotty, who was 'it,' slapped Oakley on the shoulder."

"You're it!" he called out triumphantly, laughing as he ran off.

Oakley frowned. "See what you made me do! Now I am 'it' and you are going to have to wait." He ran off after a screeching little girl and caught up with her quickly. He tagged her on the arm. "You're 'it', Larissa!" Oakley grinned as he ran up to Teddy. "Okay, now we can go explore!"

The courtyard was a wonderful place to look around, and for an hour, Teddy and Oakley romped through the high grass, peeked under rocks, and climbed up stairs. They looked out from the top of the castle wall, and admired the view that overlooked the canal that drifted lazily far below them. The water twisted and turned like a snake, winding around the gigantic mountainous cliff bottoms. All too soon,

Margie noticed they were up along the wall and called them back down where they would be safer.

They would have liked to go into the castle and investigate what was in there, but after they had finished praying, Brock had instructed everybody to stay outside while he looked around for a place to sleep. As usual, Mark and Henry had gone in with Brock to help him search. The courtyard was alive with lots of little bodies running around, screeching and having fun. The last couple of days' trials of fear and hunger seemed to vanish for the moment.

Teddy and Oakley were sitting at the bottom of the steps they had climbed up, pondering where they should explore next. Teddy leaned back, peered along the side of the steps, and noticed a door handle. He stood up and pulled on the latch. The door swung open, and Teddy peeked inside the little room under the stairs. The light from the sun glimmered on something inside, and he opened the door wider. He let out a shriek and jumped back.

"What is it?" Oakley asked. He stood up and came to Teddy's side. "Wow!" he said, "It real knight's suit!"

Teddy looked again and was relieved to discover he had not seen a person standing there, but a suit of armor. He let out a loud sigh of relief. "I thought there was a mummy in there!"

Oakley grinned back at Teddy as he went into the tiny room. Teddy shrugged off his friend's look as he followed Oakley and replied, "Well, I did!"

They found a narrow cot in the corner, with a small table next to it. "This must have been where one of the guards lived." Oakley commented. He reached up and took down the helmet, blew the dust off, and put it on his head. Teddy laughed at his pal as Oakley tried on the rest of the suit. He could barely move after it was all on.

"That must have been how David felt when he put Saul's armor on!" Teddy chuckled. A strong gust of wind blew up, and at the same time, they heard a sound from the forest that made the hair stand straight up on their necks. The door of the room slammed shut and both boys jumped back in fright. Oakley struggled to pull off the helmet as Teddy felt around for the doorknob. He yanked the door open, and heard Margie calling. Oakley stripped off the rest of the armor and together they ran out of the room, back into the courtyard with the others.

"Margie, did you hear that howling noise? What was it?" Teddy found he was not the only child shivering with fright. The little ones, some crying, some white with fear from the chilling sound, surrounded Margie.

"Sit down everyone! Please! I can't talk when you are climbing all over me!" Margie pried four-year-old Kia off her foot and set her on the grass near Tina. Kia quickly hid her head in Tina's lap. Brock, Mark, and Aaron came out of the castle's big wooden double doors and ran over to the little group.

Brock quickly surveyed the group of wide-eyed children and turned to Margie for an explanation. He had heard the sound too, but inside the castle it had not sounded so loud. "Margie, what happened? Is everyone okay?"

"We heard a horrible sound come from the woods! Whatever could have made that noise?" Margie stood beside Brock with eyes wide with fright. Brock put a finger to his lips, reminding her to remain calm in front of the little ones. The last thing they needed was to have their leaders break down in an emotional mess. Margie understood the gesture and closed her mouth before she got herself into any more trouble.

"Now, listen children, I know this is all new to us, and we have no idea how far we are from civilization. My guess is that is was just an animal that lives in the forest, and he was making a call to another one of his friends. We will be safe inside this castle. I will shut the door so nothing can get in, okay?" Brock went over to the wheel that held the large door and began to turn it. Mark ran over to him to help.

"But Brock, you got in when that door was shut!" Scotty, the tester of the group, could not help putting his two cents in. Brock gave him a look that said, "Don't say any more!" Scotty clamped his mouth shut and shrugged. He was not scared of any old animal.

With the door sealed tight again, Brock approached the group and told them what he had found inside the castle.

"There was a kitchen with a few old pots and pans, and some utensils, but there wasn't any food. I also found some rooms we can use for sleeping quarters, but they will need some cleaning. There is a lot of old hay, dirt, and cobwebs everywhere." Margie nodded as Brock continued, "Okay, everyone, here is what is going to happen. Margie, you take the girls with you and go clean up inside. Mark and Aaron, you go beyond the wall and see if you can hunt down some fruit or berries for us to eat. Do not eat anything until you have had it checked by Margie or me. I don't want you dying from food poisoning out there, got it?"

"Yes, sir," they answered. Brock went over to the door and cranked it open just enough for the boys to slip under and go off hunting. "Be careful!" Brock called after the two of them. They waved back in response as they crossed the drawbridge.

Brock turned towards Margie and saw her frowning at him. "What's the matter?" He asked her.

"You sent them out there alone when there is a 'who-knows-what' running around waiting to eat them alive?"

"Margie, don't worry about them. They are strong boys, with good heads on their shoulders. I am sure they will be careful. I don't think you have to worry about a thing. Besides, I don't think it was an animal. It was just the wind."

Still not persuaded, Margie turned away, not in the mood to argue. Brock had taken responsibility of the group, and she wanted to trust him. She only hoped he was right and that she was doing the right thing.

She left Brock and called to the girls to follow her. As they approached the door, she called back to Brock, "Make sure you watch the others!"

Brock raised his hand acknowledging he had heard her, and then realized that he had not told her what to do to "turn the lights on" inside. "Margie!" He called to her as she entered the castle.

Margie's head peered around the corner again.

"I did not get a chance to tell you about the glowing walls yet. Touch the walls as you walk down the hallway and you will get a surprise." Seeing her unsure look he reassured it would be fine.

Puzzled, Margie disappeared around the corner again, and walked down the hallway. A greenish-blue light filled the corridor, and she found the other girls crowding around each other staring at the glowing walls. "What is it?" Tina asked curiously.

"All Brock said was to make sure we touched the walls as we came in. He said he would explain to us later what makes the light."

They continued down the short hallway, which had a door on either side, and came out into an enormous room, with a tall staircase directly in front of them. A magnificent chandelier dangled from the second floor ceiling high up over the staircase, though no light was coming from it. The girls stared in wonder at the grandness of the first floor, wondering what lay beyond the long staircase; but even with the glowing light from the rocks, the room still had many shadows and corners that were dark and spooky. The girls did not dare venture out into the large room, fearing they might run into something very scary. Tina voiced the question they were all thinking, "What if there are some wild animals hiding in the rooms somewhere?"

Margie assured them it that would not be possible for anything to have come in because of the sturdy, secure walls that surrounded them. "Okay, girls, let's check out some of these rooms and see if we can find a place to rest our weary bodies." She turned back down the little hallway they had just come down, and looked into the first door she came to. It was a room filled with wooden benches and a long table, with large logs cut for legs.

"This looks like the dining room." Margie announced. "We won't clean this room yet, but we'll focus on the rooms for sleeping. We need that the most."

"And food!" a little voice piped up in the middle of the group.

Margie smiled. "Yes, Lissa, food is needed too. I hope the boys find something good to eat, and soon!"

The door across from the dining room turned out to be the kitchen. Margie would have liked to look around to see what neat things she could find, but pushed the thought out of her head in order to concentrate on what was important. They entered the "grand" room again and looked into the two doors nearest to them, deciding they would use these two rooms for sleeping quarters. Margie made sure they had good, solid doors for keeping out any critters that just may have made it in. She just did not feel like snooping around too much in the darkness, not having the proper lighting. Deep inside she was terrified at all the unknowns that lay ahead of her. She prayed and asked the Lord for strength to stay strong for the others; if she lost her head in all this, there would be no end of keeping the children from getting frightened.

They discovered that both rooms had a fireplace and some rustic looking couches made out of twisted branches. Margie had seen a similar piece of furniture made once in her town, when she had turned four years old. Her father had taken her on a special birthday trip to see a furniture maker, and together they watched the man work on a little rocking chair. He had to steam the pieces of hickory saplings and then put them into a form to keep their shape. When they were dry, he had clamped them together and added piece after piece until it was finished. Margie's father had surprised her by saying the little chair was her birthday present. She had loved rocking her dolls in that chair and wondered what had become of it after the train accident that took her away from her home and family.

"Margie, what should we do first?" Tina's voice broke through her thoughts bringing her back to reality. Margie looked at the floor covered with old, musty hay - it needed a good scrubbing. There were probably bugs and even mice living inside all that dust and grime.

"Let's start gathering up the old hay and take that outside. We can get the boys to collect fresh grass, and we can lay it on the floor to help keep any drafts out.

Tina walked over to the handmade chair and picked up an old pillow that was lying on top of the seat. A dusting of feathers floated out from a hole chewed in the side by a little critter. The girls started laughing as they caught the feathers and blew them at each other. Margie knew the feathers would make an even bigger mess, but she let the girls have some fun knowing it would help ease any tension they were feeling.

CHAPTER FIVE

Let There Be Light!

While the girls were inside cleaning the castle, Brock was outside giving the boys instructions in cleaning the yard. He was hoping they would uncover some interesting treasures, though if they found *anything* he would be happy. They did not have much to begin with, except the clothes on their backs and a Bible. They also had two pails, along with the knife the sailor had handed Brock as he was leaving the burning ship, but the food and water they had found under the lifeboat's seats was long gone. They needed as much as they could find. He went outside the castle walls and found a fir tree. He showed a couple of the boys how to make brooms for Margie by breaking the branches off, leaving the little needles for bristles.

When everyone was busy with the jobs he had given, he decided it was time to go back down and see what he could make out of the underground river he had discovered in the cavern below the castle. He left Scotty and Oakley in charge of the boys outside and hurried into the castle. He went through the kitchen and pulled open a door hidden behind the fireplace. Closing it behind him, he carefully made his way down the steep steps. He felt a little guilty leaving the boys alone, and he remembered Margie's admonition, "Make sure you watch the others!" but he excused his actions by reasoning that what he was doing would benefit the whole group. He might find something useful down there that could help them out in a big way! He only hoped Margie would see it from his point of view when she found out he was not outside in the courtyard with the younger boys. His stomach rumbled in hunger as he reached the bottom step, but he ignored it as the glowing dots in the river attracted his attention. At last, he could see some of God's wonders of creation up close!

He walked over to the pond and knelt beside the water. The little flashes darted about in the water, leaving little streaks of light behind them. He scooped some of them up in his hands; the little specks were so tiny he could barely make them out, but grouped together, they made a brilliant glow. Brock figured they had to be living creatures the way they swam and squiggled. He stood up and glanced at the lab door; maybe he could find out more in Mordecai's laboratory. On his way towards the door, he studied the river and noticed that on one side, it seemed to be flowing in from under the wall. He turned and went closer to the wall. Upon closer investigation, Brock found there was a very thin space where fresh, clean water could stream in from outside, and connected up with the river inside. He realized the little glowing dots were not in the water flowing inside, but were only in the water already in the dark, underground channel. The idea of going to the laboratory faded as he became intrigued with this new discovery. He began walking in the opposite direction, and discovered that the trail of the river twisted and turned throughout the belly of the castle. It snaked along the cold, moss-covered stone walls, and seemed to go on for an eternity. About one hundred feet down the path, Brock came to a stop when he saw a large water wheel which had a pump, lots of gears, and many long pipes sticking out. The pipes stretched out from the pump to the inner wall of the castle where they disappeared inside. Without hesitation, Brock quickly stepped into the cool water and began cleaning out the leaves and sticks that had piled up around the wheel. He did not mind getting wet, though he was not sure if he liked having the "creatures" swimming around his legs. He hoped they did not think he was their dinner.

When he had most of the mud and leaves cleared away, Brock slowly began to turn the long metal handle attached to the wheel. The giant wheel groaned as it struggled to life after years of being unused. Brock stepped back once it continued to turn on its own and watched as it began to rotate a little faster, picking up the glowing water in its wooden pockets that sat every twelve inches. A rumbling sound on his left startled him, and he turned to see the larger of the gears starting to turn. A second gear connected to the first began to spin and the big pump let out a hiss and a pop. Brock ran out of the water and stood on the other side of the river, afraid the whole thing was going to explode any minute. After a few minutes of watching and waiting, everything settled into a pattern and seemed to be working fine. He mustered up his courage and slowly approached the massive machine again and examined it closer. There were brass and glass pipes sticking out of the pump as if it was a pincushion. The water that the wheel scooped up poured into a deep basin under the pump, and in turn, the pump sent the water into the pipes. Each glass pipe glowed with the luminescent water and disappeared into the wall of the castle. Whatever he had done had activated the main mechanism of power for the castle. He could not wait to go upstairs and see what was going on up there!

* * * * * * * * *

Meanwhile, Margie was busy helping the girls finish cleaning the last room. The brooms the boys had made had come in very handy, and she was glad Brock had thought of the idea. She began to feel guilty for being angry with him earlier that day, and asked the Lord to forgive her. Brock had simply been doing his job, and had been gone so long because he was trying to get in, and out, of the castle. Besides, he was outside with the boys right now, helping them clean up the yard. She could not stay mad at him for long.

A popping sound startled her and she jumped, nervously turning towards the noise. The other girls stopped what they were doing and looked fearfully at Margie.

"What was that?" Tina asked her knuckles white on the broom handle.

Suddenly, little bursts of light began to shine from behind some metal shutters.

Margie frowned as she took a step towards the wall, where she could hear a little bubbling sound. "What in the world?" she said aloud. She saw some little hinges on the metal flaps, and gently lifted one. To her amazement, she noticed some glass pipes set back in little recesses along the walls. Each one had a clear fluid inside with lots of little glowing specks in it. The ends of the pipes disappeared in either side of the walls. The pipes were glass outside of the walls, but became brass as they retreated behind the stone next to it. Each little "window" had a metal shutter that could open or close, depending on how much light was needed. It was simply ingenious! Who would have ever thought a medieval castle would have lights! Then the thought occurred to her, "We are not alone! Somebody lives here and they turned on the lights!"

A commotion outside the door caught Margie's attention. Oakley ran into the room panting from excitement. "Margie! Come quick! Teddy fell out of the tree and he's hurt his leg real bad!"

Margie took off with Oakley not far behind. "Is Brock with Teddy now?"

Oakley shook his head. "I don't know where he is. He left me and Scotty in charge when he went off exploring."

The anger began to well up in Margie again. "How long has he been gone?" she asked sharply and immediately felt bad when she saw Oakley wince at her tone.

"For about an hour now." he answered quietly.

Margie found Teddy sitting up with his back against the tree and he was whimpering softly.

"What happened?" She asked as she took his foot gently in her hands and began to flex it back and forth, checking for any breaks or sprains.

"I found a baby bird on the ground, and I wanted to put him back in his nest. I didn't think the nest was so high."

She smiled tenderly at him as she gently set his foot down.

"Your leg isn't broken from what I can tell, just sprained. You must have twisted it when you landed. We will wrap it up for a few days, and you will have to take it easy for a while. No more climbing trees or running around until it is healed. Okay?"

Teddy nodded in reply.

Then as an after thought she asked, "Did you get the bird back up to his family?"

Teddy broke out into a grin. "I sure did! His mother was so happy to see him too!"

Margie knew how important it was to all the children to see families reunited. After all these children had been through, they appreciated seeing families with mommies and daddies. She held her hand out to him. "Here, I will help you inside. Just lean on me, that's it, go slowly now."

Teddy put his arm around Margie's waist and kept his left leg off the ground as they began to hobble towards the castle door. Just then, Brock came bursting excitedly out of the castle doors, almost knocking the two of them over.

"Margie! You'll never believe what I discovered! It will be such a blessing to us...." His excitement faded as he took in the glaring look Margie was giving him. "What happened to Teddy?" His forehead wrinkled in concern.

"If you had been out here watching the boys like I asked you, this would never have happened. He fell out of the tree and sprained his ankle." She did not feel like talking to him.

Brock sensed the anger in her voice and decided to keep silent. He gently took Teddy's other arm and together they helped guide him into one of the newly cleaned rooms. They set him down on the fresh, sweet-smelling grass they had spread, and Margie helped him get comfortable.

"There, that should do it." Brock said as he stood up. Looking around the clean room, he commented, "The room looks great, girls. Did the boys come back with some food yet?" The recessed lights caught his attention, and he was surprised at how much light the glowing pipes gave off. He was eager to tell them about the water wheel and pump he had found, but decided to wait. He could sense Margie did not care to discuss it right now; for some reason she seemed extremely agitated, and he had no idea what had caused her anger.

Margie ruffled Teddy's hair as she answered Brock. "I haven't seen the boys. I hope they are all right." She glanced towards the door with a worried look. "Maybe you better go check on them."

Before he could say anything, the two food hunters returned with the front of their shirts overflowing with fruit. "Dinner is served!" they called.

Eleven children hungrily grouped together on the floor, and after a quick prayer of thanksgiving for their food, they all dug into the sun-ripened fruit, and filled their empty bellies. Mark explained how they had discovered rows of untended fruit trees, with lots of fresh, ripe fruit hanging on each. A few overgrown gardens were also nearby, which had lots of pumpkins, squash and other vegetables just waiting to be picked, if you had the patience to wade through all the weeds.

Finally, after two long days of being away from the *Haven,* they all settled down with full stomachs, resting comfortably in the knowledge that their Lord, Who had taken care of them thus far, would continue to watch over them.

CHAPTER SIX

Settling In

It took a couple of days for the orphans to settle down in their new surroundings. Margie tried hard to establish a schedule they could follow so that she could keep order in the large group of children. There were many different personalities and each one needed comfort and love. Margie found herself becoming worn out being the mother of nine younger children. Because she knew it was important to find her rest in her Lord she began each morning with prayer and quiet time. Since they only had one Bible, she read from it every other day, while Brock took it on the other days. She knew this time was vital to see her through the long, tiring days of trying to survive in this strange land, but she also enjoyed the quietness of the morning with the birds singing in the trees. She liked to sit under the tree in the middle of the courtyard, and imagine the castle to be her personal mansion in heaven with Jesus sitting on His throne close by, until a biting bug brought her back to reality of the present day. Still, it was nice to dream what the Lord had in store for her in heaven, though she still wanted to get a chance to grow up some more, marry, and have a family of her own some day.

When her devotions were done, Margie would set off for the kitchen to see what she could whip up for the hungry children to eat. She did not have much to work with, just the fruits and vegetables the children gathered the day before, but nobody was complaining – they were all just thankful they *had* s*omething* to eat.

Brock also got up early and had his own quiet time with the Lord, since he too needed the Lord's strength and wisdom to see him through each day. He read from the little Bible every other day soaking in every bit of comfort and guidance he could find. He never knew what to expect during the day from the children, and even the castle itself had enough mystery to drive him to his knees, along with that strange sound that continued to break the silence of the forest around them.

The children woke up around seven every morning, and the first thing everyone did was have breakfast, and then have devotions together. Brock wanted to make sure their spiritual life was full, and he wanted to be the best leader he could possibly be. Mr. Carver had begun this ritual on the ship coming across the ocean on their trip to Florida, and Brock wanted to continue it, though he knew he could never take Mr. Carver's place.

Margie made a big deal of setting the long dining room table with the utensils she had found in the kitchen. They used large shells for plates, a chipped bowl for serving the food, and some tin cups she had found stacked on a shelf for water. It was not much, but to her it felt a little bit like home back at the orphanage. She wanted to recreate the atmosphere of the orphanage as much as she could to help the children adjust to their life now. There were times when she yearned for their comfortable home back in Boston, where she did not have to worry about a thing. Margie had been responsible for some of the cleaning and caring of the little ones, but at least she had not been in charge of everything.

It was a little overwhelming having all the responsibility on her shoulders. True, Brock was the real leader, but he did not know anything about housework or taking care of the children's' needs. Ever since they had found land, she always seemed to be upset about something when it came to Brock's decisions or actions.

She was not sure why, but she wondered if she blamed him for their separation from the *Haven*. Maybe if he had been watching more carefully this would have never happened.

As Margie set the bowl of chopped fruit in the middle of the table, she folded her hands and asked the Lord to take any bitterness out of her heart. She hated the feeling of unrest it brought and wanted the heavy feeling to lift.

"Margie? You okay?"

Margie jumped at Brock's voice. She saw him watching her from the doorway.

"Oh, hi, Brock, I didn't know you were there."

He studied her carefully. "You never answer my questions these days. Is there something wrong between us? You always came to me before with your concerns." He walked over to her and placed his hand upon her folded hands. "Margie, you are like a sister to me. I would never do anything to hurt you." He spoke the truth, and she knew it deep inside. He was the perfect example of how Paul instructed Timothy to be in First Timothy 5:2. Tears of shame filled her eyes. She quickly pulled her hands away from his and wiped the drops away.

"I know, Brock. I am sorry for the way I have been treating you. I have been blaming you for what happened, and I need to ask your forgiveness. It was wrong for me to think that way. It wasn't your fault." She looked guiltily up at him. There was not any hint of anger or resentment in his clear, blue eyes. He smiled, and she noticed for the first time how much of a beard he had been growing over the last couple of days. It was short and stubbly.

"Of course, I forgive you, Margie. I can understand why you felt that way. I was supposed to be in charge, and I failed in many ways. I must ask your forgiveness too, for running off and leaving the boys a few days ago. I was so eager to find out more about the luminescent creatures. You must admit, the light has been a big help, hasn't it?"

She shrugged as she turned away. "Sure it has. But it would have been a big help too if you had discovered it the next morning."

Brock did not feel forgiven by those words. He took her arm and turned her around to look at him. "But *do* you forgive me?"

Margie nodded as she looked into his kind face. "Yes, Brock, I forgive you." She pulled away again and walked towards the door.

"Margie, promise me one thing."

She stopped and waited. "What is that?"

"You must always come to me with your concerns. There is no telling how long we will be here, and we need to be able to talk, or else we will have the longest days, or I hate to say- years-of our lives."

Margie nodded in agreement. "Okay, Brock. I promise." Deciding to change the subject she asked him, "What are your plans for today?"

"I am going to take the older boys out, and we are going to check out the cave opening I saw from the drawbridge the other day. I think there might be a trail leading down there."

Margie looked fearfully at Brock. They had not gone very far the last couple of days except to venture out for food and wood, which they had no problem finding in the orchard. The old pump in the courtyard provided all the fresh water they needed, so why did they need to explore any further? What was Brock thinking?

"We will be fine, Marg. We will stay close and not go too far."

"But what about tha-that sound?" They had heard the strange, eerie howling a few more times since the day they had arrived. It seemed like every time the wind blew strong, it disturbed whatever it was, and it began to howl loudly.

"Oh, that sound is nothing but a wild dog howling at the moon."

"Dogs don't howl at the moon during the day." Margie was cutting up some more fruit, her back to Brock.

"True, but I still don't think it is anything to worry about."

"All right, I will trust you. But if anything happens to you, I don't know what I would do!" She felt a quick squeeze on her shoulder as he walked by.

We'll be fine. I am going to go wake the children."

* * * * * * * * *

A few minutes later a band of sleepy-eyed children came wandering into the dining room and found their seats on the benches that lined each side of the table. The seats were not very sturdy, just some planks placed precariously over some large, thick stumps; but they served their purpose. After breakfast, Brock led devotions with the children still sitting at the table. Afterwards, the girls helped Margie clean up and another day of excitement began.

Standing with Teddy and the girls, Margie waved goodbye to Brock and the troop of boys as they headed off to explore some of the island. She was glad Teddy was staying so he could rest his sprained ankle. Teddy's foot was much better, but she wanted him to continue to take it easy and not do a lot of hiking in the mountains. She closed her eyes and prayed for the boys' safety, feeling a little uneasy about their leaving the castle. She tried to put it out of her mind as she turned to the children who were eagerly awaiting her instructions. There were many rooms to explore in the castle, and Margie had taken the lead to investigate them. She was hoping to find a sewing room or a large closet with some clothes left behind by the original occupants of the castle.

"Today, I think we are going to go upstairs and check out the rooms on the second floor. We really need to find some blankets and clothing so we can make sure we are properly covered at all times."

It was very cool inside the castle and became even colder at night when the sun went down. The fires Brock made put out some heat, but the chimneys needed cleaning and the smoke became unbearable at times. Brock had retrieved the tarp from the lifeboat, and they used that for some of the children to sleep on, but that did not keep out the drafts from the stone floor. Margie wanted to find warmer quarters to sleep in, but was not sure she would find anything better since the whole castle was made of stone. They had not discovered anything of interest in their exploration down-stairs; except for a few faded and dusty tapestries they found hanging on the walls. They had taken those down, and after a good scrubbing, they used those for their blankets during the night. Not much else remained in the rooms. It looked as if someone had picked them clean, and all that was left was cobwebs and echoes of voices.

* * * * * * * * *

Margie slowly made her way up the creaky steps, brushing away the cobwebs as she went. The monstrous chandelier hanging over their heads from the second floor ceiling was all lit up with glass tubes filled with the glowing water. It lit up the stairway, revealing a few boards with holes on the edges. Margie steered the group away from the treacherous wood.

Tina was at the back of the group, making sure there were no stragglers. She watched Teddy as he carefully made his way up the stairs, favoring his sore foot. "You okay, Teddy? This isn't too much for you, is it?"

Teddy paused as he turned around to answer Tina, holding onto the wobbly rail for balance. "Yes, I am fine. It doesn't really hurt too much anymore."

"All right, but just don't do too much."

Teddy nodded and turned away as he began his ascent again.

"What if someone lives up there?" Larissa asked loudly enough for Margie to hear.

Margie turned around and smiled encouragingly at Larissa. "Oh, Honey, if someone lived up here, he would have introduced himself to us long before now." Her little bit of humor did not get the reaction she had wanted. Margie smiled sheepishly as they reached the top. She took a quick glance around and noticed that some of the metal shutters were closed making the hallway appear very dark.

"Tina, you take Kia and Larissa with you and go to the left side of the stairs. Teddy, you come with Blossom and me. We will check out the door that is in front of us. Tina, make sure you open up those shutters as you pass them in the hallway."

The little group disappeared down the dark hallway. A flicker of light broke through the blackness as Tina opened up one of the large shutters. A cloud of dust blew into her face setting her off in a coughing fit. Slowly Tina, Larissa, and Kia made their way around the stairway. It was in the shape of a square, overlooking the downstairs with a crumbling banister all the way around. Whoever had built the castle had left a lot of open, empty space. There were windows set back in little nooks in between the rooms, but they only allowed in a little light since they were so small and narrow.

Margie took Blossom's hand in hers and made sure she stayed close by her side. She was only three, and Margie did not want to think of what would happen if they lost her inside the huge castle. Walking up to the bulky door, she tried lifting the latch but found the door would not open. She pushed on it with her knee as she lifted the latch, but it still would not budge.

"Teddy, stand back with Blossom as I push on this door. Don't let her out of your sight!"

Margie pushed against the door with all her might, but the door remained stuck.

"I wonder what's in there?" she thought aloud. "Someone wanted to leave it locked for some reason." She looked closer and noticed a tiny keyhole underneath the latch. She knelt down and peeked into the hole. She saw a stream of sunlight shining in from a back window, revealing some sort of chest underneath. "Now I *really* want to check out that room. There might be something in there that we could use." she commented.

"What did you see, Margie?" Teddy asked, peering inside the keyhole.

"I think I saw a box."

"What do you think is inside it? A body? Maybe it's a tomb where they buried dead people."

Blossom's nose wrinkled up and her lip quivered. "No dead 'eeple. I 'cared of them!"

Margie quickly hushed Teddy with one look. "No, Blossom, don't worry. Jesus is watching over us and there is nothing to be afraid of."

Blossom ran over to Margie and lifted her arms up for Margie to hold her. Margie picked her up and Blossom buried her face in her shoulder. "Shh, there now, Honey. Margie won't let anything happen to you."

The sound of footsteps echoed close behind them and they turned around. Tina's group stood there with forlorn looks on their faces.

"Nothing?" Margie asked.

"Nothing of interest, but we did find some more tapestries hanging on the walls. What did you find?" Tina asked.

"Nothing either. This door is locked, and we can't get in. Maybe when Brock gets back he can pick open the lock. Was there anything else worth looking into?"

Tina nodded. "There are some more stairs leading up at the back end of the hall in one of the nooks with a window. Maybe there is something upstairs."

Margie agreed, but decided they had looked around enough for the morning. "How about we all go outside into the courtyard and I'll tell you a story?"

A chorus of cheers erupted from the group, and they all happily trudged down the steps, into the bright, warm sunshine where they settled down on the grass to hear one of Margie's stories.

CHAPTER SEVEN

The Cave

B rock and his group of boys were happily doing what they loved the most, exploring the countryside with the sun on their backs. The castle was remarkable, but they had not found anything interesting in it, as of yet, and so they were eager to find something exciting outside. They crossed the drawbridge and combed the edge of the cliffs searching for a way to get down below. When they did not find any way down, Brock had them go back over the drawbridge, and look along the ledges surrounding the castle.

It did not take Brock long to find the old, rotten trap door along the same side of the castle that he had found the hidden entryway into the cavern. He had not gone this far in his search before; and therefore, he had never seen the trap door. He moved some of the dead leaves and branches out of the way and pulled up the soft wood that crumbled in his hands. There were some stairs chiseled out of the rocks down below. One by one, they climbed through the hole and followed the stairs that twisted around the edge of the rocks and out of sight of the drawbridge.

"This must have been an emergency exit when invaders came." As usual, Brock was leading the way, making sure the path was safe.

"Isn't this grand?" Scotty remarked to Oakley, who was cautiously making his way down the steep steps.

"It makes me nervous," Oakley muttered, as some loose stone went sliding out from under his foot and splashed into the water below. "I'm scared of falling! Do you think it's deep?"

"Sure it is." Scotty said. "It's the ocean - full of creepy, crawly eels and things. You would never make it out alive. There is probably a shark down there, lurking around for something soft and squishy to eat." He smacked his lips, imitating a hungry shark.

"Cut it out, Scotty!" Brock called behind him. "We don't need your foolish comments right now. I will send you back, and you can stay with Margie if you aren't going to behave."

"Sorry," Scotty muttered. Under his breath he added, "Boy, can't a guy have any fun around here?"

When they reached the last step the slope of the trail lessened a little, though it still wound down to the bottom of the mountain. They pressed along the edge of the rocks, not wanting to take any chances of falling over, just in case there *were* some sharks waiting to eat them. The pathway suddenly ended and they found themselves staring at a giant rock blocking the trail.

"Hmmm...I wonder what this is for." Brock took a step closer and touched the rock. He saw some symbols on the front, but he could not make them out. A gust of wind blew up, and Brock cautioned the boys to step back so the wind would not knock them over the side. A familiar sound made them freeze in their tracks. It was the wild howling sound, which grew louder and creepier as the wind blew harder.

The blood drained from the boys' faces and panic began to set in.

"Wha-what was that?" Oakley asked grabbing Brock's arm.

"Sounds like it's directly in front of us," whispered Mark, who was also standing next to Brock. The wind died down and the howling stopped. Brock remained where he was, unsure of what to do next. He remembered telling Margie they would be fine and did not want to break his word. She must have heard the sound too.

"Brock, maybe we should go back." Aaron looked nervously towards the trail that led back to the castle. "I am sure whatever it is will want to eat us for dinner."

Brock decided it was time to act the leader and remind the boys Who was watching over them. "Now listen, guys, we have a God with us, Who is stronger and more powerful then anything on this earth. He created every living creature, and He gave us dominion over all the beasts of the earth and fowls of the air. Yes, we need to be cautious, but we also have to trust the Lord in all things, and do what we need to do to survive. Now, are we going to be men of God and continue on?"

Oakley and Aaron both seemed a little unsure, but seeing the others were not turning back, they decided to save face and go on too, but to where? The path was blocked!

Brock seemed to be convinced there was something they were missing. He studied the rock and looked in the bushes next to them, going in as far as he could. He disappeared in the brush, leaving the boys wondering if they should follow. All of a sudden, they heard him say, "Aha!" and crowded close to the spot where he had gone.

"Stand back!" he called. "When I pull this lever the stone should move."

They stepped back, careful not to fall over the edge, and watched as the stone slowly rolled to the side pulled by a large cable. An opening beyond the stone revealed a cave behind it! Brock came out of the bushes and brushed the leaves off his pants. "Follow me, boys!" he called behind him.

They hurried after him and found themselves in a large open cave in the shape of a horseshoe. The path went around to a little sandy beach that met the water, about ten feet away, with an opening on the other side of the cave where the water led out into the canal. There were two old, rotting boats on the edge of the shore and two more pulled up onto the sand.

"Those boats might come in handy some day," Brock commented, jumping down from the ledge onto the sand. "We can work on the boats and fix them up."

Brock glanced at his pocket watch. "It is time to head back for lunch. We don't want to be late or else Margie will worry."

"Girls," grumbled Scotty. "They never let you do anything. Always worryin', always bossin' you around…"

Brock was growing impatient with Scotty's comments. "Scotty, now listen to me; the only reason Margie worries is because she cares about us. She needs us as much as we need her and the other girls. Moreover, you had better make sure you obey her when she tells you something, or else you will have to answer to me. Is that clear?"

Scotty nodded to make Brock happy, but deep in his heart he was still miffed. "No girl is going to tell me what to do," he thought to himself. "I'm nine years old and I can take care of myself! I would run away if it wasn't for that howling sound." He paused a moment and glanced behind him at the water lapping near the edge of the cave. He thought again about the creepy, crawly eels and things that lurked in the water just below the cliff they had climbed down earlier. He was brave, but then again he was not willing to be someone's dinner. The running away idea would have to wait for another day.

Scotty was the last boy out of the cave and silently watched Brock seal the stone over the entrance. He waited for Brock to start on before him, and deliberately lagged behind as they climbed up the steep slope; just close enough to remain in the safety of the group, but far enough away to be alone.

* * * * * * * * *

Larissa was sitting with her legs pulled up to her chin, her thin plaid skirt pulled over her knees. She was listening intently to the story Margie was telling about Jonah and the whale. She had heard it before, but it held more meaning to her now. She knew what it was like to be in a big storm and to have to go over the side of a ship. True, they did not have to go into the belly of a whale, but being under the tarp in the lifeboat was bad enough. She was thankful they had found land when they did. A movement caught her eye, and she turned towards the gate of the castle. Brock had left it open so they could easily get back in, and she saw a shadow of something just beyond the large door. Through squinted eyes, Larissa peered closer, trying to make out the shape. The shadow turned and she saw a little face looking back at her. When the child saw that Larissa had noticed her, she turned around and ran away. Larissa jumped up.

"Margie! I just saw somebody!" She pointed to the opened gate.

Margie glanced to where Larissa was pointing. She did not see anything. She stood up and walked over to the gate, looking around the corner. There was nobody there. She frowned.

"Are you sure you saw somebody, Larissa? It might have just been a shadow from the sun."

Tina went over to Margie. "It may have been one of the boys playing a trick on us. It was probably Scotty trying to tease and scare us again."

Margie thought for minute. Scotty did have a reputation for teasing the others, and he had been unusually good for the last few days. She would not be surprised if he was up to one of his tricks again. "Okay, girls, I am sure it wasn't anything. Let's sit back down and finish our story."

It was not long before the group of boys did come marching back into the courtyard, eager to tell the others what they had discovered in their searching. Brock let the boys tell everything and went over to Margie to see how they had fared.

"Did you find anything of interest?" he asked her.

She shook her head. "The only thing we found was a locked door. The rest of the rooms were empty, but Larissa claims she saw someone looking in from the gate while I was telling them a story. Did Scotty happen to leave your group at all?"

Brock knew where she was going with her question. "He never left the group. He gave me a little bit of trouble in the cave, but stayed at the back the whole time. He never got in the lead at all. There was no way he could have been who Larissa saw."

Margie swallowed hard. "Did *any* of the boys ever leave the group?" She was hoping he would say yes.

"I'm sorry, Margie, but none of the guys were ever out of my sight."

"Then who was it? Maybe we are not as alone as we think."

"I can't imagine why they wouldn't be using the castle if there was someone else here."

Margie had a thought, but felt a little nervous telling Brock. He would think she was a wimp, but she said it anyway. "They probably did not want to get eaten by the big, howling creature."

Brock was going to laugh, but saw how serious she was. He smiled at her and replied, "This castle would keep out the strongest of animals, Marg," he said gently. "We are safe behind these walls."

As she turned to go back to the group of children, Brock silently prayed for their safety, hoping beyond all hope that he was right, and she was wrong.

CHAPTER EIGHT

The Little Visitors

The next morning, Brock rose up early and spent more time praying during his quiet time with the Lord. Ever since Margie had told him about the stranger's face looking in at them, he had felt a heavy burden to pray fervently for the orphans' safekeeping. He was not sure what it all meant, and if the stranger was even a threat, but he wanted to make sure that he was right with the Lord before heading out that day. He had plans to bring the lifeboat into the canal near the castle, and anchor it on the sandy beach in the cave they had found the day before. The other thing he wanted to do was go down to the lab in the 'cavern' and look through some of the papers and bottles that were all over the room. He wanted to find out if there was any information on who had lived here, and what had happened to them.

Hearing a sound at the doorway of the dining room where he sat, Brock glanced up from his Bible reading. Margie stood in the doorway with a worried look on her face.

"Did you see Blossom this morning?"

Brock shook his head. "She's not in her bed?"

Margie stepped into the room. "When I woke up this morning the door of the girls' room was open and Blossom's spot was empty. I was hoping she was with you." She wrung her hands in despair. "Oh, where could she have gone?"

Brock stood up. "I will check outside. Maybe she went into the courtyard." Deep inside, he doubted his words because the main doors were too heavy for a little girl of three to push open.

"I will check the kitchen," Margie said, "Maybe she was hungry." She rushed out the doorway and ran across the hall to the kitchen calling Blossom's name.

Brock found the doors of the castle shut and locked. No little girl had gone out those doors. He went down the hall towards the stairs in the main room, lifting up the metal shutters that covered the glowing tubes so he could have more light. He had made it a habit to close the shutters every night so the hallways would not be inviting to any curious children who might wander off. He saw that his idea did not work very well, what with the missing baby and all.

As he rounded the corner behind the stairs, he heard a little noise. He stopped and listened carefully. It was the sound of a child crying. He hurried behind the stairs and found a small entrance going underneath the stairway. He knelt down and peered inside the pitch, black hole. Not able to see anything, he hesitantly reached in and felt around. One of the sidewalls began to glow at his touch, and as his eyes adjusted, he could make out a small shape in the middle of the closet-like area.

"Blossom, is that you? Are you all right?" He crawled into the tight hole and found that there was more room once he got through the door. Blossom turned towards him and held out her arms.

"Kitty!" she cried, clutching her little arms around his neck.

"Where's the kitty?" he asked, gently patting her on the back.

"Scatch me!" she sobbed, holding her arm out in front of his face. Not being able to see very well in the dim light, he scooted back to the opening and told her to go through first.

"No!" she screamed. "Kitty!"

"But the kitty is not nice if she scratched you." Brock said. "Now go out and I will be right behind you."

The little girl did not move. Getting a little irritated, Brock tried to pry her arms away from around his neck. She had a strangle hold on him! "Blossom, let go of me. I need you to obey me and go out the door."

"No!" she screeched again.

"Brock! Where are you?" He heard Margie's voice coming from the other side of the wall.

"I'm in here! I found Blossom! Can you coax her out the door?"

Margie followed their voices and bent down at the front of the entrance. "What in the world did you find, little one?" She asked, as she reached in for Blossom. Blossom glanced towards the back of the closet before she let go of Brock's neck and let Margie pull her out of the room.

Once he was free, Brock turned around to get a better look at the room. Two yellow eyes stared back at him from one of the dark corners.

"Nice kitty," he said as he slowly made his way backwards towards the door. He was not sure what the animal was, but he was not interested in finding out while he was trapped in that whole!

Margie watched as his long legs came out first and then Brock's head appeared. She could not keep back the chuckle that slipped out, simply from relief that everyone was okay.

"What did you see?" she asked.

"Eyes." Brock answered.

"Was it a bear?"

"Too small." He brushed the dust from off his pants. "I wonder why that room is under there. I couldn't see if there was anything else inside - it was too dark. I will have to check that out later with a light."

Suddenly, a little ball of fur went racing out of the hole, brushing against Margie's skirt. She screamed and leaped back in fright. The animal raced down the hall, with Brock not too far behind. It ran into a mound of rubble along the edge of an outside wall and disappeared. He stood looking at the pile for a few minutes, rubbing his stubbly chin in thought.

"Brock, what was that thing? Was it a cat?"

He nodded his head. "It sure looked like a black cat to me. Obviously it was wild seeing how frightened it was. We better check out Blossom's scratches she said she got from the 'kitty.'"

They went back to the kitchen, and Margie sat Blossom down on the wooden bench in one of the corners. As Margie examined the marks on the girl's arms and legs, Brock stirred up the coals to get the fire going again.

"They don't look too bad, but I want to clean them out as best I can. Could you please put a pot of water on to boil?"

Margie sat down next to Blossom and took her hands. "Where did you find the kitty?" she asked her.

Blossom pointed towards the door. "Out dare. I 'erd a noise at door. I open door and see kitty."

"Did you follow it?"

"Yep."

"And the kitty hid in the room under the stairs?"

"Yep."

She pulled her hands out of Margie's and stuck her thumb in her mouth.

Brock came back with a pot, and Margie picked up a piece of cloth from her pile on the table and dipped it in the hot water. She had ripped one of the tapestries they had found into little strips and used those for washing. She tested the water on her arm before putting it on the little girl's skin. Blossom whined a little as the water stung the wounds, but Margie sang a little song to get Blossom's mind off what she was doing.

The loud sounds of footsteps echoed in the hall as the children raced for the dining room.

"Sounds like the children are up," Margie commented. "But what am I going to feed them? I haven't had time to prepare anything!"

Brock had an idea. "Let's go out and pick our food together this morning. Then we can sit down on the grass, and we can have devotions outside!"

Margie nodded, and Brock went off to pass the idea onto the others. By the sound of their cheers, Margie knew it was a good one.

Half an hour later, all the children had had their fill of sweet, ripe fruit. The fruit trees in the orchard close by the castle were still loaded with delicious fruit, even though they had not been tended or pruned for many years. Brock gave them a few minutes to run around in the cool morning sun, knowing that the heat of the day would come too soon. The sun got very hot by mid-afternoon, and they had to stay inside until the intense heat died away.

"All right, everyone! Let's sit down and start our devotions now!" Brock called.

As the group came panting back to Brock and Margie, they settled down on the grass in front of them, laughing and chattering happily. Blossom came over to Margie and climbed up onto her lap, and Kia and Larissa settled down on either side of her. She smiled as the children quieted, and Brock began his lesson.

"I will be reading from Matthew 21 today, about the owner of the vineyard who lent it out to some keepers to take care of." He began to read in verse 33 about the parable of the vineyard, and how the master of the vineyard traveled to a far country; when it was time for the reaping of the fruit, he sent some servants to gather the harvest, but the keepers of the vineyard beat them and sent them away. After sending a few more groups of servants, he finally sent his son, hoping they would have respect for the master's own son. They did not, cast the son out, and slew him. After reading the parable, Brock looked up. "Who is the Master they are talking about in this story?"

Oakley raised his hand. "They are talking about God."

"Right," answered Brock. "And who are the servants?"

"Missionaries like Mr. Carver." Teddy said.

"Good, Teddy! And who is the Master's son?"

"Jesus!" A group of voices rang out together.

"Exactly! Jesus was sent to save us from our sins and the people rejected Him. They killed Him, hoping they had finally done away with Him. But did He stay dead?"

"No!" they shouted together.

"Right! A few days later, He arose and showed Himself to His disciples. Jesus had to die and rise again so we could have a Savior, to rescue us from hell..."

* * * * * * * * *

Brock's voice floated across the orchard to where another little girl sat, soaking in all the words he said like a sponge. He talked about a Savior, someone who could rescue them! The words echoed repeatedly in her head, giving her hope for the first time, that maybe there was Someone who could help her people. She had seen the despair in the elders' eyes, and known ten years of fear and torment. If this Savior could rescue them from hell, then He was surely Somebody she wanted to meet! She heard the young man say he was going to pray, and when he said the word, "Amen" the children all got up and headed back into the castle courtyard. She watched and waited, hoping they might keep the massive gate open. When it did not close, she slowly got up and approached the drawbridge.

* * * * * * * * *

The little children raced around the courtyard, playing tag while Brock sat playing Mancala with Mark. Suddenly a voice called out in fear, "There's that face again!"

Brock quickly ran over to the gate of the courtyard and looked around. He saw a small, bare foot disappear around the corner of the castle. He raced out after the child and saw her far ahead as he came around the side.

"Stop!" he cried. "Don't go! We won't hurt you!"

As the little girl ran around the other side, he turned back hoping to head her off before she crossed the bridge again, but she never came around from the back. Sending Mark and Aaron to one side, he went on the other side, thinking maybe she had gone through the trap door, but the wooden door remained untouched over the hole. At the rear of the castle, he noticed some brown hair dangling from a bush. He looked up the steep mountain cliff and saw a little shape looking down at him from the top, and then she disappeared.

Back inside the courtyard, Brock closed the gate. He did not know who the little girl was, but if she told others they were here, there was a chance they might not be friendly.

They were safe for now; at least that is what Brock hoped.

CHAPTER NINE

Sunday

The sun was shining brightly the next morning, but the air was cool and refreshing. A little breeze blew up now and then, and the tree branches moved as if they were waving to the children. Once again, Brock took the children outside into the orchard to read God's Word. He had decided the night before that since it was Sunday, they were going to have a morning worship service, and then relax for the remainder of the day. Everyone had liked the idea, and they all were looking forward to a quiet day. Almost a week had gone by since they had last seen Mr. Carver and the *Haven*. The fire had broken out on Monday night during the storm; here it was Sunday, and still there was no sign of Mr. Carver, or anybody else for that matter, to come and rescue them.

* * * * * * * * *

Margie sat down behind the children on the soft grass, so she could keep an eye on them while Brock led the service. She also kept an eye out for the little girl stranger that seemed to keep appearing off and on. Brock began their service with a prayer, and then asked if there were any special requests for songs. Hands lifted up high, and Brock pointed to Larissa.

"What do you want to sing?"

"Haven of Rest."

Brock began to sing, and a choir of voices soon filled the air as the children joined in.

* * * * * * * * *

As the clear, childish voices rang out through the orchard, the melody floated across the forest, through the green leaves of the tree tops to where another little girl sat alone. The music caused her to sit up straighter; the sounds were lovelier then anything else she had ever heard. She jumped up and began running to find where it was coming from. She had never heard anything so sweet in all her ten years. She raced through the woods, hoping she could find it before it stopped. It was so different then the low, wailing of the shell that she knew. It grew louder as she approached the orchard, and with her heart beating fast, she tiptoed behind a tree and peered around. She saw all the strangely dressed children sitting on the grass, and to her surprise, she found the sounds were coming from them. It was so beautiful! The words that were coming forth brought tears to her eyes:

My soul in sad exile was out on life's sea,
So burdened with sin and distressed,
Till I heard a sweet voice, saying,
"Make Me your choice";
And I entered the "Haven of Rest"!
I've anchored my soul in the "Haven of Rest,"
I'll sail the wide seas no more;
The tempest may sweep over wild, stormy, deep,
In Jesus I'm safe evermore.
I yielded myself to His tender embrace,

In faith taking hold of the Word,
My fetters fell off, and I anchored my soul;
The "Haven of Rest" is my Lord
O come to the Savior, He patiently waits
To save by His power divine;
Come, anchor your soul in the "Haven of Rest,"
And say, "My Belovèd is mine."

When the song ended, the man in front turned some pages in his book and read, "He stilled the storm to a whisper; the waves of the sea were hushed...and He guided them to their desired haven. Psalm 107:29-30. Those are wonderful verses to remember in this stormy part of our life. God is our haven and we are right where He wants us to be, safe in His care." The group was silent as they soaked in the words that he had spoken. Then he asked for another request and a little boy raised his hand. He pointed to him and then another melody, just as sweet as before echoed from their lips:

"When upon life's billows you are tempest tossed,
When you are discouraged, thinking all is lost,
Count your many blessings; name them one by one,
And it will surprise you what the Lord hath done.
Count your blessings, name them one by one;
Count your blessings, see what God has done:
Count your many blessings;
Name them one by one; count your many blessing
see what God hath done."

The words ran through the girl's head – count your blessings, when you are discouraged, thinking all is lost...didn't that describe her and her people? What had they left to live for? The despair, the gloom, and the fear...it all seemed to melt away as she sat behind the tree and listened to the song. When the pretty music died away, the man stood up and began to talk again, reading from a little black book he held in his hands. It looked like the Journal of Mordecai, from which the elders read every night before retiring to their mud huts. She listened as he talked about a boat, and a man named Mr. Carver. She did not understand all that he said, but as he went on, a feeling of compassion for these lost children crept over her. It was a feeling she had learned to suppress, in order to survive on the island with her people, but however hard she had tried to still the feeling, it would always come back stronger then before. She felt sorry for these children, and saw that they were hurting inside just as she was, but they seemed to have a hope that she did not have.

Again, the young man turned some pages in his black book and read, "Therefore I say unto you, Take no thought for your life, what ye shall eat, or what ye shall drink; nor yet for your body, what ye shall put on. Is not the life more than meat, and the body than raiment? Behold the fowls of the air: for they sow not, neither do they reap, nor gather into barns; yet your heavenly Father feedeth them. Are ye not much better than they?"

He kept on reading, but his voice trailed off as the little girl's mind pondered all that he was saying. Who was their heavenly Father? How did He feed them? Did He come and visit them when they were inside the fortress? She shuddered, remembering the words of Mordecai: "Take care that you never enter the fortress, or else you will suffer the bewitching curse of King Farrell. His spirit will float down and haunt you for the rest of your life, taking revenge for the greedy men that took his life."

She focused on the man's voice, hoping to drown out her terror.

"But seek ye first the kingdom of God, and his righteousness; and all these things shall be added unto you. Take therefore no thought for the morrow: for the morrow shall take thought for the things of itself. Sufficient unto the day *is* the evil thereof."

He stopped reading and was silent for a minute. "God has been good to us, and we have no reason to complain. I know we are alone, without Mr. Carver's guidance, and I must admit I get scared at times, but even if Mr. Carver were here, we would still have to pray that God's will be done in our lives. Our God, Who is also our King, is always with us, and He said that He would never leave us nor forsake us. He's watching over us and is taking care of us."

The girl raised her head and looked around. Where was this person he was talking about? If He promised to never leave them, why couldn't she see him? Maybe their King had died just as King Farrell had many years before, but instead of haunting them, he continued to help them.

A twig snapped beside her and she leapt up, ready to sprint away. She looked up into the gentle face of a young woman, about the same age as her own sister, Mariah. The little girl's legs trembled in fear.

The woman smiled gently and in a quiet voice said, "It's all right. I won't hurt you." She paused a moment and continued quietly, "Would you like to come and listen?" She held out her hand and stood silently, waiting to see what the girl would do.

The girl stood as if ready to run at any second.

"If you want to stay here and listen, that is fine." She put her hand down and started to turn away, then stopped. "My name is Margie. What's your name?"

The little girl looked down at her dirty, bare feet, and at the same time, she noticed the woman's feet, which were red, bruised and covered with scratches. Her forehead wrinkled in thought. Where had Margie come from anyway? Was land that different away from the island? She looked curiously up into Margie's face, and then turned away shyly as she answered quietly, "I am Nettle."

Margie thought she misunderstood the name. "Did you say Nellie?"

The girl shook her head. "No, Nettle." She was not sure how much she should talk to this kind woman, so she stepped back. "I must go." She turned away.

"You are welcome to come and listen any time you want." Margie smiled at Nettle. "I am sure the other children would love to meet you."

Nettle glanced longingly towards the group, who had by now, all turned around to watch. She suddenly felt frightened and turned away. "I must go." She ran off into the forest.

Margie walked back to the waiting children and looked at Brock. "Her name is Nettle. What an odd name indeed! Isn't it strange that she speaks English just as we do? I wonder where she lives."

Margie sat down again, but could not keep her mind on the rest of the service.

Brock finally said the last prayer, and then gave the group permission to run around, as long as they stayed within calling distance. He sat down next to Margie and stretched out on the grass, closing his eyes as the sun beat down on him. The warmth spread over his body, and it felt good to relax. He opened his eyes and squinted up at Margie, who was staring at him. "Something wrong?" he asked.

She shook her head. "No, not really; I was just thinking."

Uh oh, Brock knew that meant trouble. He turned over onto his side and leaned on his elbow. "About the little girl Nettle?"

"Yes, about Nettle and who her parents might be. Where did they come from? I was also thinking about Mr. Carver. I wonder where he is now, and if he is looking for us."

Brock had thought about that a lot the last few days, and he wondered if the *Haven* had even made it through the storm and fire. He shrugged. "If he *is* still alive he is looking for us."

Margie's eyes brimmed with tears. "*If* he is still alive? I hate when you say that!"

Brock replied gently, "Remember how he sent us off the boat during the fire? He told me that he needed to stay in case they couldn't put out the fire because the sailors weren't saved yet. He wanted to make sure they had the opportunity to get saved in case they were in danger of losing their lives. He was always thinking of others first."

Margie sniffed. "I know. He was kind and good. Do you remember the first time he came into the orphanage?" she laughed, brushing a tear away with her hand. "He came into the room with that silly hat on! He couldn't even make it through the doorway it was so tall!"

Brock laughed as he remembered that day. Mr. Carver had come into the dining room, wearing a very large hat. As he came through the door, his hat hit the top of the frame and fell over backwards. He had hidden candy in the hat and it spilled all over the floor, much to the surprise of the children. They had been delighted when he had said; "Come and get it!" and they had scrambled around grabbing up all the sweets. Candy was a rare treat for them! When they had found all the pieces, he had told them a story about a man Who had come to save them from their sins; and that man, Jesus, was offering them a free gift of salvation to anyone who wanted to take it, just like he had offered them the free candy.

Mr. Carver had come back many times, telling them more stories about the wonderful Jesus-Friend of his. Teddy was the first to receive the Lord into his heart, and over a period of a year, more and more had turned their hearts over to the Lord.

Not long after that wonderful year, the Talleys were given a notice of foreclosure and had to close down the orphanage.

It had been a sad day when the lanky, tall man had come, once again, to present the Talley's with a notice of payment due. It had happened a few times before, but they had always found the money to make their payment. This time the money was not found soon enough and the government had finally closed it down. Some children had been sent out west on the orphan trains, to find families to settle down with. For the rest of the group, it was decided to sail them down to a newly established orphanage in Florida. Heartbroken, the children cried when it came time to say goodbye to their beloved Mr. and Mrs. Talley. Mr. Carver had been granted permission to sail with the eleven down to Florida, and he gladly took charge of them all. His home was in Florida, where his wife waited for him, and he knew of some families in his church who might adopt some of the children. He arranged for the *Haven* and its crew to sail the children to their new home. It was while they were on their journey to Florida they became separated from the master ship.

Margie's smile disappeared as she thought about what would happen to them if Mr. Carver never found them. She felt a gentle squeeze on her shoulder and looked up into Brock's stubbly face.

"We will be fine, Margie." he said soothingly. "Someone will come for us. Remember what I read today? We do not need to worry about our future. Who knows, maybe God sent us here for a reason. Only time will tell."

She gave him a little smile. "Thank you, Brock. That is very encouraging. What would I do without you?"

Brock looked into her eyes and then quickly turned away. As he stood up he said, "I am going to check on the others. I am sure they're getting hungry by now." and with that, he ran off.

Margie frowned, wondering at his abruptness in leaving. Did she say something she should not have said? "Lord, help me be wise as a serpent, and gentle as a dove," she prayed.

"Please help me sort out these feelings of mine. My moods change so quickly, I never know what I will be feeling. Also Lord, help me be content with whatever Your will is for our lives. In Jesus Name, Amen." She felt better after she took her troubles to the Lord and got up to join the others.

CHAPTER TEN

Scotty's Discovery

The door slammed behind Scotty as he ran out into the courtyard with an angry scowl on his face. He looked around for a good place to hide and spotted the door under the stairs leading up to the wall. Glancing back to make sure no one had followed him, he raced over to the other side of the yard and yanked opened the door. Looking back one more time, he quickly squeezed himself through the narrow opening and shut the door behind him. Finally, he was alone and away from the constant rebukes of Brock and Margie. The tiny room was dark, but Scotty knew the room well. It had been a favorite place for the children to play, each taking turns trying on the suit of armor and pretending to be a knight. He felt around for the table and cot he knew were in one corner of the room, and when he felt the rough canvas of the bed, he sat down and stretched out on the tiny cot.

Once settled in the safety of the darkness where nobody could see him cry, the angry tears began to stream down his face. "It's just not fair," he thought to himself. "Why must Brock always yell at *me*? He hates me! I know he does! Why else does he always pick on me?"

Bitter thoughts swirled through his head, as he roughly wiped away the tears. "Why did my dad have to leave me? Nobody ever loved me! My momma had to die before I was old enough to remember her – she must not have loved me either. Brock keeps preaching how much God loves me, but I know it's a lie. God doesn't love me or else He would have answered my prayers by now."

The thought of running away seemed good to Scotty, but he stayed where he was on the little cot and squeezed his eyes shut. He was too tired to get up, and he figured it was a good enough hiding place for the moment. Slowly he drifted off to sleep, his face relaxing as he dreamed of his mother, imagining her to be alive and well.

An hour later, Scotty woke with a start and sat up, not remembering where he was. His eyes slowly adjusted to the darkness, and he could make out the outlines of the table next to him. He suddenly remembered that he was inside the guard's house, hiding from Brock and Margie. "Can't a guy have any fun?" his thoughts began where they had left off before. "All I was doing was sliding down the banister. I used to do that at the orphanage all the time! Seems like all I ever do is get yelled at around here."

He stood up quickly and accidentally knocked over the little table next to the bed. He bent down to set it up upright again, and his foot knocked against a loose stone underneath the table. Pulling the table farther away, he knelt down and shoved the stone to the side. He could feel a small gap underneath, big enough for his hand to fit inside. He stood up and quickly opened the door of the room so he could let some light in. The sun streamed in and shone down on the hole he had found. He pulled a smaller stone away and discovered a leather pouch in the dirt underneath. He gently pulled it out, not knowing how fragile it might have become over the years, and leaned back against the bed frame. He carefully loosened the top of the pouch and pulled out a yellowed piece of paper. It looked like an old map! He studied it long and hard, realizing someone had carefully mapped out the entire castle on the piece of paper. A dotted line began at the guard's house and stopped at place inside the mountain behind the castle. A little notation on the third floor drawing said, "Door to tunnels."

Scotty's heart beat fast at his newly discovered secret. How exciting to have a map all to himself!

Hearing faint voices in the courtyard made Scotty leap into action; he quickly but carefully slid the map back into the pouch, and hid it away in the hole, placing the rocks over it. He had just set the table in place and leaped onto the cot when Brock appeared in the doorway.

"There you are, Scotty. We were wondering what had happened to you." He paused and looked away for a minute before asking, "May I come in?"

Scotty nodded but did not say anything. Brock stepped through the narrow door and had to duck to keep from hitting his head. "I have never been in here," Brock commented. "It must have been for the king's guardsmen. They probably took turns sleeping in here after each shift change."

Brock ran his hand through his sweaty hair, making it stand straight up. It was time to find a way to try to cut it. He knew he was starting to look shabby and ill kempt. He briefly wondered what Margie thought of him and then turned his attention back on the present situation – Scotty. "We were worried about you, Scotty. You ran off, and we had no idea where you were."

"You probably didn't even look for me. You're just saying that to make me feel better."

"Oh, we looked for you all right. We searched all the rooms of the castle, and it wasn't until Teddy told me about this room that I came out here to check. When I saw the door open, I figured this was where you were hiding. Pretty neat place too."

Scotty did not reply, but kept his back turned towards Brock.

Brock prayed for the right words to help Scotty. "Scott, listen, I know I was a little hard on you today, and I'm sorry. I was frustrated with the project I was working on, and I took it out on you. Will you forgive me?"

Scotty shrugged. "You always seem to take it out on me. Why are you asking forgiveness now? Besides, you aren't my dad. I don't have to listen to you."

Brock sighed. "No, I'm not your dad, but I am the one in charge. If Mr. Carver were here you would have to listen to him, but he isn't. I am the one responsible for all of you children, and I am going to be accountable for your actions and mine."

"I was just sliding down the banisters. What's wrong with that?"

"It wasn't the action that was wrong. It was the safety of it. I am not sure how strong those banisters are, and I did not want them to crumble under your weight. You or somebody else for that matter might have been hurt."

"But you didn't have to yell at me," mumbled Scotty.

"No, I should not have yelled, but I was worried that you would fall at any minute. I was concerned for your safety, and, you did not listen the first *or* second time I told you to get off. I had to get your attention. Besides, I already asked you to forgive me. You can't hold a grudge forever for my mistakes. I'm human too – I'm not perfect."

Scotty turned and looked at Brock. Brock truly seemed sorry and his face showed genuine worry on it. Scotty decided it was time to go back. Besides, he was hungry and did not want to miss supper.

"Okay. I forgive you." Scotty stood up, ready to leave the tiny room. It had grown somewhat stuffy and he wanted to get some fresh air.

"Do you have something to say to me?" Brock asked.

Scotty frowned as he pushed his toe around in the dirt. "Yeah, I guess so. I'm sorry for not listening, Brock. And I'm sorry for making you worry."

Brock smiled and reached out to muss Scotty's sweaty hair. "All is forgiven. Now let's go tell the others you are okay." He put his arm around Scotty and together they went back to the castle, but Scotty did not forget his precious discovery. He made a silent vow to go back and investigate the map later on.

* * * * * * * * *

Nettle waited behind the tree in the orchard for an hour, hoping to see the children that afternoon, but the gate never opened. She figured they were working inside, and she yearned to go and help them. She had never been inside the castle before, but that was because her parents and the elders of the village forbade her from going in there. She had heard many stories about King Farrell haunting the castle, and though she did not totally believe they were all true, she did not want to test her theory. All the elders believed and respected all that Mordecai had written sixty years ago – his words were their law. If all he said was true, then maybe the children were not ever going to come out of the castle again. Maybe King Farrell had slain them all in their sleep! She shuddered at the thought and tried to think of better things.

Time passed slowly for Nettle, though she was in no hurry to go back to the village. She was spending more and more time alone these days, searching for something more meaningful in her life, and she had a feeling these children had what she was looking for. She was not sure how to go about getting it though, because she was afraid to speak to them. The other children of the village were not kind to her and teased her continually, and she was not welcomed into their games and play. She had been marked ever since the day she had been born, and her father claimed it was the mark of the devil. She hated the small spot, which was high up on her arm, and her mother always made sure the sleeves on her dresses were long enough to keep it covered. Her father was always finding some way to punish her, and she was convinced her father did not love her. She longed for a friend and therefore continued coming to the castle grounds in spite of her father's warnings and beatings. Besides, what else did she have to do to pass the time?

CHAPTER ELEVEN

The Villagers

Deep in the woods, on the other side of the island, three men sat around a low wooden table on soft grass mats in the middle of a crude hut. Their shelter was simple, made out of branches, mud, and dried grass. A cast iron pot hung over a small fire and the aroma of warm stew filled the room.

Raul, a menacing looking fellow, with long black hair, dark eyes, and a body built like a mountain was speaking, "I tell you, Bryan, the pirates have returned! I have seen life at the castle, and who else could it be but Bone's and his gang of bandits?"

"I can't believe after all these years they would suddenly just come back." Argued the red haired man named Bryan. "Our lookouts have been watching the newcomers since they came, and their reports are that they are just children."

"Bah! It's a trap! That is exactly what they want us to think! Mordecai warned of these men returning – his writings can't be any clearer for us to understand. They want what we have and will use any means to get it!"

Bryan stared into the fire, as if waiting for an answer to come. The sparks flew high as Matthew poked the log with a stick.

"You haven't said anything, Matthew." Raul commented. "What are your thoughts on all this?"

Matthew turned, his long gray beard shaking from the movement, his old, wrinkled forehead furrowed up in thought. His answer came slowly, from a mind full of wisdom and a mouth empty of teeth.

"We need to watch them. They might be children, but the pirates may be luring us out. We need to tread carefully."

The hopelessness on the other men's faces was evident. The years of hiding had paid its toll on them and they felt worn down. Maybe it was time to just come out and get it over with.

"Maybe we can fight them," Raul suggested.

Matthew turned. "What do we fight them with, Raul? They would have guns and swords. We have nothing but sticks and a few sharp stones. The few knives we have can barely skin a rabbit anymore."

Bryan brushed his red hair out of his eyes. "We should just go down there and surrender to them. Just give them what they want. Why do we need it anyway?"

Matthew's eyes blazed with anger. "We will not give them anything! They are greedy men and will do evil things with it. If we fight them, we will all die. There will be nothing left of our village! They didn't hesitate to kill King Farrell did they? We will make a plan and stick with it. We will obey Mordecai's word and stay away from these people. And if there is anybody out there who dares defy Mordecai's words, then he will be punished!" His meaning was as clear as a bell. If Bryan tried anything funny, he would pay a high price.

Bryan shuddered. He knew Matthew was not joking. "I understand," he answered.

A rustling sound came from the grass mat that covered the door of the hut. A woman's face looked around from behind. "May I come in?" she asked softly.

"Enter," Matthew growled, upset at the interruption.

The woman who entered was young and pretty, with her long, brown hair flowing softly over her shoulders. She bowed her head in respect at the men and waited for them to address her.

Raul spoke to her. "Sadie, I have told you before not to come in here and bother me when we are in meeting. What is it you need this time?"

With her head still bowed, she blinked back the tears of hurt at her husband's sharp tone. She got a hold of herself and spoke quietly, "Your daughter has run off again. I think she went to the fortress."

Raul's face turned white and then red. Leaping up, he banged his fist on the table. "I thought you told that child not to go there! Why don't you keep a better watch on her?" He raised his hand as if to strike her. Seeing her flinch, he decided against it. Now would not be a good time to discipline her. He could do that later.

Matthew spoke a command to Raul. "Sit, Raul. I will take care of the matter." He was Sadie's father, and he did not like to see her husband treat her so roughly. He would have given her to another man, *if* there had been another man for her to marry. The people of the island were getting few and far between. He wondered if there would come a day when there was nobody left.

Reluctantly, Raul sat back down, but Sadie could feel his stare boring into her back. She knew she would get it after the sun went down. Didn't he always come home in a raging temper after dark? He spent hours working on his 'seaweed' wine, and even more hours drinking it. She wished he could find something else to do to pass the weary hours.

Bryan felt the tension in the air and spoke, hoping to break the heaviness. "I will go find the girl. I think I know where she has gone."

Matthew's eyes squinted at Bryan in suspicion. "You aren't planning on turning us in, are you?"

Bryan shook his head. "No, sir, I promise to go and bring back the girl. I won't do anything else."

"Permission granted." Matthew sighed as Sadie moved aside for Bryan to walk out the door. As Bryan pulled aside the mat, he glanced over towards her and their eyes met. She knew the angry look on his face was not meant for her, but for her husband who treated her so unkindly. Bryan was Sadie's older brother, and he loved her dearly, and would do anything to protect her. Her eyes darted away, afraid that Raul might see the look that passed from brother to sister. Bryan understood the gesture and after taking a quick, glaring look at Raul's back he went out the door.

* * * * * * * * *

Bryan carefully made his way through the brush, not making a sound as his bare feet treaded lightly over the sticks and leaves. He knew the trail well, and could travel it with his eyes closed if necessary.

Seeing the villager's 'sentry' standing up on his lookout station, Bryan turned off the main path and climbed up to visit with his friend Kato. Kato was a young man of seventeen years of age, and he had just finished the two-day wedding rituals to Nettle's older sister, Mariah. Matthew had forced them to marry, saying they needed to have as many children to populate the diminishing number of people on the island. They only had eighteen people left as it was. What they needed was new life, and with Kato and Mariah being so young, they should have many children. He hoped that

Kato was not like Hugh who had no children with his wife Rosa after being married two years!

Kato turned at the sound of approaching footsteps. Bryan gave him the sign of two palms down, which was the signal that meant he came with no demands. Kato waved him up and Bryan climbed the rock, which looked down upon the top of the castle. Bushes shielded them from being seen from down below, but the view was spectacular from where they sat.

Bryan was the first to speak.

"Any changes?" He looked down into the courtyard and saw little dots running around as if they were chasing each other.

Kato shook his head. "I don't see why we have to spy on them so closely. They are just children. What harm can they do to us?"

"Matthew and Raul seem to think they are the descendants of Bruno. He thinks it is a trap. I don't see how it could be, but he is the leader. He thinks he is high and mighty being a distant relative of King Farrell." He slapped his leg in frustration. "I just want to get out of here. There has got to be more to life then living here, dying from absolute boredom."

Kato looked at him. "Are you planning something?" His brown eyes sparkled in excitement. He had the same feelings as Bryan. He did not like being tied down to a woman he had to take care of for the rest of his life. Mariah, the name of his new wife, meant bitter, and that was what she was; she was not pleasant to be around. Why else did he take the job of lookout all day, and all night if he could?

"Kato, how long has it been since we went into the fortress?"

Kato shrugged. "About two months I think."

"Too long I say. We need to get in there and spy on them closer. We need to listen to their conversations and see if they do plan on ambushing us."

"But Bryan, you know Matthew forbade us to ever go in there again. What about the curse of King Farrell?"

"Curse…smurse! That's just a story Mordecai made up to keep us out of there. We have been in there many times and nothing has happened. Those children have been in there for the last two weeks and nothing has happened to them! What do we have to fear? We know all the secret tunnels, and we can listen to them without them even suspecting we are there. Let's do it…tonight at the full moon. You will come with me?"

Kato looked unsure, but agreed after Bryan playfully punched him in the arm. "Great. Meet me here at dusk."

"What do I tell Mariah?" Kato knew he would never hear the end of this one. He had only been married for three days and here he was planning on running off during the night.

Bryan frowned. "Sneak off after she is asleep, then you won't have to hear her complain. Now I need to go get Nettle. She is down there again. Maybe she knows something we don't. See you tonight."

Bryan waved as he left Kato to his surveillance. He made his way down the mountain and crept to the edge of the woods. From where he was, he could see Nettle standing behind one of the trees in the orchard. He whistled loudly, making the sound of a bird call. Nettle's arm lifted in acknowledgement, and then she disappeared into the brush. He knew she was making her way down the path that had become overgrown with weeds over the years of being unused. He waited patiently for her to appear, and when she did she was breathless and pale.

"Am I in trouble?" she asked, taking his hand and walking with him back towards the village.

"Your father was very angry when he heard you were gone again. Nettle, why do you insist on running away? Do you like the beatings your father gives you?"

Nettle hung her head. She did not answer. Bryan stopped and stooped down in front of her. He lifted her chin. "I know the yearning you feel in your heart, little one. I have it too. The desire to fly away like a bird is so strong it almost hurts."

She looked up at him with tears in her eyes. "Uncle Bryan, I hate the beatings I get, but there is something these children have that I want! They have such peace, and they talk about a Savior that helps them live and make the most of their lives!"

Bryan frowned. What Savior could they mean? Were Bone's ancestors aiding them in their life on the island? Nobody had seen a ship, or any other life for that matter. What was Nettle talking about?

Seeing the confusion on her uncle's face Nettle continued, "A Savior Who they claim never leaves them. He died and rose again – He is their God."

Bryan felt a shiver run down his spine at her words. He feared she would get in bigger trouble if she ever mentioned those words to her father, Raul.

"Nettle, listen to me – you must stay clear of those children. They only mean trouble for us. Do not tell your father anything you told me or else you may not live to see tomorrow. Do not live up to your name and be a nettle in his flesh, do you understand?"

He could see the confusion in her eyes, and she looked as if she wanted to argue, but she gave in and nodded. "Yes, Uncle Bryan. I won't mention it again." However, in her heart, she talked to the God of the strangers and asked Him to work out this whole situation. "If You *are* real," she prayed, "then reveal Yourself to my father so I don't have to do it."

* * * * * * * * *

Bryan waited on the rock, overlooking the peaceful landscape below bathed in the soft moonlight of the full moon. He grew impatient as time ticked by. Kato should have been here by now! He wondered if that nagging wife of his had found out his plan and locked him up. A snap in the brush made him jump. Kato walked onto the rock and Bryan sighed in relief. "Where have you been?" he demanded.

"Mariah wouldn't go to sleep. She stayed up working on one of her baskets. How many does a woman need anyway? We have about fifty of them already! There isn't any more room in the hut for another one." He grumbled in misery.

Bryan slapped him on the back. "Oh, come on; grow up. Act like a man. If you treat her with kindness, she will treat you with kindness. My Buttercup makes the baskets too, though not as many now that baby Tomas takes up most of her time. Let her alone and let her make her baskets if that makes her happy. Come, and let's go to the lab."

A little while later, the two men found themselves deep in the cavern of the castle. All was quiet since the orphans had long since retired to their rooms. The men found the pumps running, and the water wheel turning. It surprised them to find that the children had discovered the secret of making light in the fortress. It deepened their suspicions, thinking they had knowledge of the fortress from stories passed down by Bruno and his relatives. They crossed over the rocks and went to the door of Mordecai's old lab. They found it slightly ajar and cautiously opened it. A shadow leaped out at them, and a club came down on Bryan's head. He collapsed in a heap on the floor.

Kato cried out in fear, "Don't hit me! I won't hurt you!" The shadow moved from behind the door and Kato saw Raul's great form standing there, a wooden club in his hand.

"Raul! What are you doing here?" he sputtered in surprise.

Raul scowled. "I should be asking you the same question!" he bent down to see if Bryan was all right. He touched his shoulder and shook him gently. "Bryan? Wake up! Can you hear me?"

Bryan moaned. Glancing up, he saw Raul looking down at him, and in the greenish light, his face looked like a ghost. "Ahhh! King Farrell's ghost! Don't hurt me!"

Kato moved closer to Bryan and with a reassuring voice said, "Bryan! It's okay! It's only Raul."

Bryan slowly sat up, his hand pressed on the lump on his head. "Ohh, my head! Why did you go and hit me?"

Raul stood up, glad to see that Bryan was okay, but deeply angered for their rebellion in coming into the fortress, against Mordecai's commands. "I thought you were one of the enemies. Why are you here, anyway? You have defied Mordecai's commands and entered without permission."

Kato looked at Bryan. Neither said a word. Raul's face scrunched up and Bryan quickly spoke before Raul had a notion to hit him again. "We came so we could spy a little. We wanted to look around and see if we heard anything mentioned about an attack."

Satisfied with his answer, Raul set his club on the wooden table nearby. "Well, even though the idea was good, you should have brought it to the council, and we could have sent someone better equipped for spying."

"Like you," Bryan bitterly thought, though he did not say the words aloud. Raul was in enough of a rage without adding fuel to the fire.

"Matthew will lock you up for a week when he hears of this!" Raul glanced back at the trembling Kato and asked, "Why aren't you home with your new bride?"

Kato uttered an unintelligible answer, and was happy when Raul did not press the issue.

"After you left this afternoon, Matthew and I decided we should scare the children a little bit. 'Shake them up and see what they do;. I am going to leave the key to the 'locked room' here in the lab, and see if they venture to go in. You know what will happen when they do, don't you?" Raul's mouth turned sinister with his evil grin. "I will also leave this piece of paper on the steps leading up to the main floor of the fortress. That should be enough to frighten the rest that are still alive."

He showed Bryan and Kato the slip of paper, with the words of warning scribbled on it. "Lastly, we will blow the shell from our lookout point, and they will think that the beast is going to get them for sure. Obviously, the rattling bones and whistling shells we set up are not enough."

Bryan stood up and grabbed the wall for support. Oh, how his head hurt! "What if it doesn't work?" he asked, once he regained his balance.

"It will. The words of Mordecai can scare anyone into leaving this fortress."

Bryan doubted it; they had not kept him and Kato out, or even Raul. Somehow, he felt there was something different to this group of children though he could not put his finger on it. Maybe what Nettle had told him was true, and they did have a God that was watching over them. Maybe he would find out someday if they ever met up with this mysterious group of strangers.

CHAPTER TWELVE

The Warning Signs

Margie arose the next morning and stepped outside into the courtyard for a quick morning stroll. She glanced curiously at the sky, noticing for the first time in the few weeks they had been here, that the clouds covered the sun. She did not let it worry her since she figured the plants needed to get rain occasionally to keep everything green. As she started on the second lap of her walk around the inside of the courtyard, she felt the first drop of rain hit her cheek. She quickened her pace as the drops began to fall faster. Just as she made it to the double doors leading inside the castle, the drops became sheets. She burst through the doors and startled Brock who was just heading outside. She crashed into him almost knocking him off his feet. He caught his balance, along with hers before they toppled to the cold, stone floor.

"Margie! You scared me! Is everything okay?" Brock's hands were on her shoulders, and he steadied her before letting go.

"It's pouring outside!" she laughed, shaking the drops from her hair. "I just barely made it in!" She looked at him with a grin on her face. "Scared ya, didn't I?"

Brock scowled at her. "I don't scare easily." Just as he said the words, the sound of the howling began low and long. Margie's face turned white. They had not heard it in a while, but there had not been a large windstorm for the last week either. What was it about the wind that stirred up that animal?

Margie grabbed Brock's hand. "What is that sound anyway? It frightens me so!" She squeezed his hand tighter.

Brock gently took her hand in his other one and pried his fingers free from her grasp. She blushed. "Sorry. I didn't realize what I was doing."

The sound of thunder crashed and within seconds two doors burst open and all the children ran down the hallway to where Brock and Margie stood.

"Is it a storm?"

"Are we safe here?"

"What's happening out there?"

"I heard the howling again!"

"Children!" Brock called loudly, trying to be heard above the chattering voices. "It's just a little rainstorm that's all. It's nothing to be worried about. We are safe in this big castle." He glanced at Margie. "Do we have enough food to last us for the day?"

Margie nodded. "I think so. I can try to make some fish soup with what we have left, and there is still some fruit. Maybe it will stop by the afternoon, and we can collect more for later."

"It looks like we're going to be doing some exploring around the castle today." Brock announced. There were cheers from some of the children; the others looked frightened of the idea of looking around the cold, dark castle. They never knew what they would find.

After breakfast and devotions, they all sat around the table to talk. Brock could tell some of the children were having a hard time with everything and he knew it was time for a group gathering.

"All right everyone – I have called this meeting to find out if there are any questions or thoughts on all that we have been hearing and seeing these last few weeks. I want to hear ideas if anybody has them, and if there are any fears I want to know about them too. I will try my best to answer your questions and calm your fears."

A hand reached up. "Yes, Oakley?"

"When is Mr. Carver going to come and get us? I'm ready to leave this place. There isn't anybody else here, and I was hoping we could find a mom and dad to live with. That's what Mr. Carver promised. Where are the people who were waiting to take us in?"

Brock was not sure how to answer the boy. He too had wanted to settle in with a family. He missed the closeness and the love of a mother and father. He glanced at Margie and saw she was watching him carefully. A lone tear slipped down her cheek and she did not move to wipe it away. He cleared his throat.

"Good question, Oakley. To be honest, I don't know when Mr. Carver will come to get us, or if he is even alive."

With that statement, cries of protests began, and it was all Brock could do to quiet them again. "We have no idea if Mr. Carver and the sailors survived the fire on the boat. We have to face reality, children, and realize that we may never leave this place. From what I can tell, this is an island we are on, and we are far from any civilization. We may never get off this island. What if it isn't the Lord's will for us to leave? What if He has plans for us here? Remember Nettle? Maybe there are people here who will help us out. I have been praying about going to meet them, but I haven't felt it was the Lord's timing yet. We do need clothes, and we are going to have to have more then fruit and fish to eat. Personally, I would love to have a slice of bread again. I don't know any more of surviving in the wilderness then any of you do." He looked at Margie again. For some reason he felt like he was letting her down. His heart fell and he looked away from her teary eyes. She was supposed to be helping him with this!

He tried to think quickly of an idea to help encourage them all. He thought about the few times he had sent some scouts out to a high cliff overlooking the ocean to watch for any passing ships. Each time the boys had come back with nothing to report. There was the question though about how to get the ship's attention if they *did* pass. There had to be a way to make a ship notice them! He suddenly had an idea. "Here is a suggestion: after this rainstorm is over, we will build a large bonfire on the shore near the water. We will light it and fan the smoke into the air. Maybe a passing ship will see it, and they will come and rescue us. Does that make everyone feel better? Once we get back to the mainland, we can look up Mr. Carver and find out if he is alive. If he is, I am sure he will do everything in his power to come see us. If not, then we can rest and know he is in heaven with Jesus, and we'll find new families to come and take care of us. How does that sound?"

There were nods of agreement. After that, nobody cared to discuss anything more, and Brock knew it was time to get busy. He left Margie, who claimed she wasn't feeling well, with Tina and the little girls in the girl's room to play. True, there was not much to play with, but they made do with the little sticks, stones and pinecones they had found on the ground outside. One of their favorite games was Hide-the-Pinecone. One person would hide the pinecone and all the others would go searching for it. They could go in any of the rooms on the first floor, except for the nook underneath the stairs. Coal, which was the name they had given to the black kitty, lived under there and they did not want to disturb her little hiding spot.

Brock took the older boys with him and they opened up the door in the kitchen to head to the lab. As they went down the stairs, touching the rocks along the side to activate their glow-light, a white scroll on the edge of a step caught Brock's eye. He bent down to pick it up.

"What is it?" Mark asked, leaning over Brock's shoulder to see.

Brock recognized the three symbols at the top of the thin piece of birch bark: they were the same ones carved on the rock that blocked the entrance of the cave they had discovered out by the water. Though he had not been able to make out the shapes clearly on the stone, these were very clear: one was a box with an X through the middle. The second symbol was a U with an O around it. The last symbol looked like a spearhead, with a drip next to it. The words hastily scribbled on the sheet simply said:

Leave. King Farrell haunts this place. Your bones will howl if you stay.

The boys felt a chill go down their backs. Somebody had been in the castle, and they had never even known. It left Brock feeling uneasy – he had felt safe in the castle up until this point, but obviously, they were not out of harm's way. But who would want to hurt children?

They continued down the stairs and approached the door of the lab, which was slightly ajar. Brock cautiously took the latch and began to push it open. Thinking better of the idea, he decided kicking it open would be a better approach. He pushed the door with his foot and it swung open wide. Pausing for a second, he waited to see if there was any movement. He stepped closer, the other boys trailing behind, ready to run if necessary. Brock went into the room and after a minute announced it was clear. Mark, Scotty, and Aaron slowly followed. Oakley was the last one in and since he was the shortest of the boys, he noticed the red spot on the floor near the table.

"Brock, take a look at this!"

Brock hurried to Oakley and knelt down on the floor. He touched the red spot and found it was still sticky. "Blood," he said quietly, but the boys still heard his comment. Their hearts were pounding in their chests, and they had no desire to look around the room anymore.

"Can we leave now?" Aaron was standing at the door.

"Not just yet," Brock answered. "I need to look around some more. Maybe it was just put here to scare us." Brock began moving bottles and vials around on the table. He did not find anything out of the ordinary and moved on to the shelves. He looked behind every bottle, ignoring the cobwebs that lined the shelves. "Look with me guys. See if anything looks disturbed."

Reluctantly the other four began to check the shelves, looking over their shoulders every so often to watch for danger. It was in the corner of the last shelf, that Brock found the carefully placed skeleton key. He had not remembered seeing it there before and wondered if it was for the locked room upstairs. There might be something they could use in that room, he thought. He pocketed the key so he could check out the possibility later on.

"Okay, guys, let's go up and check on the others. I don't want to leave them alone too long, what with intruders being able to come in and all."

The boys did not argue. They hastily left the lab and ran up the stairs, leaving Brock to close the doors behind him.

Back on the main floor, Brock called Margie aside and showed her the two items he had found. He did not mean to scare her any more then she was, but he felt she needed to know since she was the other responsible one in the group.

She grew quiet at his information and delicately fingered the skeleton key. Her fingernails were broken, and dirty, and her hands were red and calloused. Brock went to touch her hand, but thought better of it. He was feeling that tug on his heart again, and he did not want to do anything that might be wrong. Something had been happening inside him the last two weeks as they had been working and trying to survive together. Their hearts were being knit together through all their trials, and he knew he had to tread carefully around her. He did not view her as just a sister anymore.

Margie handed him the key. "Do you think it is a trap? Why would they just leave us a key when there wasn't one there before, *and* a note warning us that something wants to hurt us?" Another thought occurred to her. "The note mentioned bones howling…could that be what we have been hearing all this time? Every time the wind blows, we hear the howling bones of the dead who have already come in here!" She shuddered at the possibility.

Brock straightened up from where he had been leaning on the wall. "I doubt it; that's just silly. Bones don't howl! I still think it's all a ruse to get us out of here."

Larissa ran up to Brock and grabbed his hand. "Come and play hide and seek with us!"

Brock grinned at her. "Okay! You all go hide, and I will come and find you!"

There were shouts of glee as the children ran off to find their hiding places.

"One! Two! Three!"

Margie's brow furrowed as she watched Brock put the key back in his pocket. She felt a little miffed by his indifference, but tried to shrug it off. She pointed to the large rip in his pants.

"You should let me trim off the bottom." she commented.

"Four! Five! Six! What would you cut it with?" He moved away from her and headed towards the door. "Seven!"

Margie was going to suggest using his knife, but she felt frustrated at the way Brock was behaving. She turned her back on him and went over to the wooden bed the little girls slept on. She had spread the tarp from the boat out across the bed, lining it with grass, leaves and anything else soft she had found. It had taken a whole day of picking, dragging and piling, but it was well worth the effort. She had laid one of the tapestries on top of that, making a cozy little bed. It beat sleeping on the floor.

By nightfall, the rain was still coming down in sheets, and the thunder and lightening seemed to grow louder. The howling had been their constant companion throughout the whole day and they were growing weary of the sound. They finished the last of their food for dinner that night, and went to bed early, hoping the rain would be over by morning.

As Brock lay on his tapestry-bed near the door, he wondered if there would be any more intruders in the castle that night. He figured there would not be, since it was such a nasty night outside. Concerned for the safety of the children in his charge, he made the decision that when the rain stopped, he would make the biggest bonfire on the shore and try to get the attention of a passing ship. An uneasy feeling crept over him, and he wanted to leave as fast as he could. He wanted to be under the care of Mr. Carver again and leave the hard decisions up to him. Most of all though, his feelings for Margie scared him, and he wanted to be sure he remained a pure, Christian brother to her. He was not sure it was within his power to stay that way if he remained marooned on the island with her and the children.... forever. He closed his eyes as depression tried to close in on him, making him feel like a tiny, scared child.

"Dear Father in heaven please let a ship see our bonfire! Help us get away from this place! And keep us safe inside this castle." Pausing a moment, he thought of his changing feelings towards Margie and added, "Help me guard my thoughts and actions towards Margie. Give me wisdom in dealing with her, and keep me from yielding to temptation. In Your Name I pray, amen."

He slowly drifted off into a fitful sleep, the howling still echoing through the dark, rainy night.

CHAPTER THIRTEEN

The Bonfire

"Rise and shine, everyone! The sun is shining and the howling stopped! It looks like it's going to be a beautiful day!" A cheerful voice echoed through the empty rooms, and bounced off the walls, creating a reverb effect.

Margie rubbed her eyes and rolled over. The spot beside her was empty and she quickly sat up wondering where Blossom had gone. To her surprise, she found herself alone in the room. She stood up and brushed some hay from her clothes. She grimaced as she looked at her tattered dress. It hung limply on her small frame, having lost a lot of weight over the last couple of weeks. She was going to need something else to wear pretty soon if she wanted to keep herself modestly covered. Large holes dotted her skirt, and the bottom edges were frayed. There were a couple of buttons missing on the top and she had tied some grass through the buttonholes to keep her dress closed.

She shut her eyes as she remembered the day Mrs. Talley had presented her with the dress, right before they had left for the ship with Mr. Carver. It had been Mrs. Talley's gift to Margie, for all the hard work and help she had done while living at the orphanage.

Mrs. Talley's eyes had filled with tears as she hugged Margie goodbye. "Now don't you go and forget old Mrs. Talley, you hear?"

Margie had blinked back tears and hugged the woman who had become very dear to her. "I could never forget you – you have been a mother to me!"

"And you have been a wonderful daughter, and even more so ever since you took to religion. It does you good, girl – there's a hope in your eyes I never saw before. I am sure you will go far in life, especially with Brock to take care of you. Don't go passing him up for the next man who enters your life, you hear? Brock is made of good stock, and he will make a fine husband for you someday!"

A little embarrassed, Margie had quickly brushed the idea away. "Oh, Mrs. Talley, he's just like a brother to me! How could I marry my brother?"

Something else that Mrs. Talley had mentioned bothered her more, and she quickly changed the subject. "You said that religion does me good, but Mrs. Talley, it is so much more than that to me. I have a Heavenly Father Who loves me and takes care of me. I have a relationship with Him that I could never have had before if I had never given my life over to Him. Won't you come to Jesus and ask Him into your heart too?"

She looked into Mrs. Talley's old, tired eyes with a pleading look. Mrs. Talley had brushed her aside and said, "Girl, when you get as old as I am, you will have seen everything in this world. Everyone needs something to get them through the trials of life, but we take nothing with us when we go. I don't see how taking on religion will help change things now. My time is approaching to leave this world, and there isn't much more I can do to help that."

"Then you need Christ's salvation more then ever! When you die, you will either go to heaven or to hell! I want to spend eternity with you in heaven! Oh, please, Mrs. Talley..."

"Hush now, girl, no need to get hysterical about it all. I need to check on the yung'uns and see how they're faring with their packing." She paused at the door, touched by the look of concern still on Margie's face. "I'll tell you what...if I hear of anything good that happens from this religion you have, like one of those miracles that Mr. Carver talks about your Jesus doin', well, I might consider it."

Margie bowed her head in the empty castle room that day, and prayed for Mr. and Mrs. Talley's salvation, just as she had done since the day she had received Christ. She had no idea what 'miracle' might happen to show Mrs. Talley that God still ruled and reigned in the earth, but she had a sense of peace knowing that her heart was in the hand of the Lord. A loud pounding on the door jolted her out of her thoughts.

"Margie! Are you ever going to get up? We're hungry, and we are going out food hunting! Then Brock is going to build a bonfire to signal down a ship!"

Margie smoothed back her brown hair and grimaced again. Her hair felt so oily and dirty. She would give anything for a nice, warm bath! She sighed again and opened the door. Teddy stood at the door, looking like he was ready to pound on it again. Margie caught his hand in hers and laughed.

"Slow down there, buddy! I am awake now. You could wake up all of America with the noise you're making!"

Teddy's eyes clouded. "I wish I could; then someone would come and rescue us. I'm starving, and Brock sent me to wake you up. We are all out in the courtyard waiting to have devotions. Then we'll go eat and after, he said, we could go to the beach and go swimming!"

Teddy took off down the hallway and disappeared out the door. Margie walked slowly, still not fully awake yet.

She felt groggy and very tired. She wanted to turn around again and just go back to her soft little bed in the other room. Everyday was the same and there seemed to be no end of trying to survive. She wanted to just lie down and never wake up again.

A thunderous bellow sounded from outside the back of the castle. Margie froze in her steps, the sound reverberating through her very soul. The words from the note came flooding back to her, "Your bones will howl..." and her first thought was that King Farrell was coming to haunt her. The noise stopped and she waited, unsure whether to continue on or not. It left her shaking all over, and swiftly swept away the desire to stay and sleep. With wings on her feet, she flew out the door and ran right into Brock, who had been coming in to see if she was okay.

"This seems to be a habit!" he joked, but his smiled disappeared when he saw the look on her face. "You heard it too," he commented. She clung to him and he could feel her shaking all over. He bit his lip to remind him of his prayer the night before. He gently took her arms from around his waist and steered her to his side.

"It was louder this time, Brock! It was closer! It echoed through my very being! I hate that sound! I hate this place! I need to get out of here!" She was close to tears and on the brink of having a meltdown.

Brock quickly stepped away from Margie and gave her a cold look. "Margie," he said sternly, "cut that out! Just stop your complaining and accept the circumstances that God has given us. There is nothing we can do about it so get over it, okay?"

The clouded look on Margie's face disappeared as shock and hurt took its place. Brock had never spoken that way to her before! She watched as he abruptly turned and walked to the group of children who were silently waiting in the courtyard, watching the drama unfold.

Brock was quiet as he sat down on the grass in front of them. He had a hard time focusing his thoughts on the devotion he had prepared, and finally asked Mark to lead for him.

Mark eagerly jumped up and taking the Bible he began to read from Proverbs 15. "A soft answer turneth away wrath: but grievous words stir up anger…"

Brock got up and waited near the gate, far from the group so he could pray and gather his thoughts. He felt bad for what he had said to Margie, but he was tired of all the whining that the children continued to do. Was this how Moses had felt when the Israelites continued to gripe for water? No wonder Moses had struck the rock in anger! The tension of waiting for Mr. Carver was taking its toll on them all. He was trying to do right by everybody, but it was hard being the father to ten children!

He heard the children say "Amen," and looked up to see them all looking at him for instructions. Margie was still standing quietly near the castle door, head bowed and hands folded as if she were still in prayer.

"Okay, everyone, let's get some breakfast and then we can go to the beach!"

The gate was cranked open. Nine little bodies wiggled out and ran over the drawbridge. Soon they were happily picking their breakfast, and Brock was overseeing the mob to make sure nobody fell from a tree. He watched as Margie headed down the trail leading to the beach, but he did not stop her. He knew she needed some time alone, and it would do them both some good to take a breather and rest for the day.

Shouts of laughter drifted up as the children played in the water and on the sand that day. The cool, refreshing water washed away the tension of the morning just as it took the dirt and grime of the past few weeks from their badly tattered clothing and filthy bodies.

Margie made a sand house with Kia and Blossom, though unlike the first one they had built the day they landed on the beach. Kia's idea of living in a castle had changed and now she pretended to make a house like the one they had lived in at the orphanage. Margie knew exactly how the little girl felt. She reached out and brushed some hair out of Kia's eyes. "Do you want me to find a piece of grass to use as a flag?" she asked.

"We don't need a flag for our house. We need little stones to be people and animals. I will go and get some." She raced off to a little pile of stones washed up onto the beach. Margie shielded her eyes from the sun and looked towards the large fire the boys were tending. It was huge! There was no doubt about a ship not seeing the blaze, *if* there was one passing by the island.

Margie watched Brock smile at one of the boys, knowing he must have said something funny. Brock broke out into a laugh, and Margie felt bad. She had treated him terribly, and she had no right to. She knew she had been beginning to panic, and that was why Brock had spoken so sharply to her. She knew she had to apologize to him for the way she had treated him.

She stood up and brushed the sand off her dress. Her skin felt sticky and dry – it had felt good to go for a swim in the sea, washing away the dirt from her clothes and hair, but now the salt had settled in, drying her skin out and making it feel tight.

Kia ran up to her. "Where ya going? We haven't finished making our house!"

"I will be back. I need to go talk to Brock."

Kia's forehead wrinkled in thought. "Did he say he was sorry?"

Margie smiled. "Why should he say sorry? I am the one who needs to apologize to him."

"But he yelled at you!"

"Yes, but I was acting like a child. I should not have acted that way."

Kia thought for a moment and then said, "Okay. But come right back."

Nodding, Margie walked over to the blazing fire and waited for an opportunity to talk to Brock. She called his name a few times, but it appeared that he did not hear her. Losing her nerve, she began to turn away, but a voice at her side stopped her.

"You want a stick to poke the fire with?" Brock offered her a long stick. She shook her head. "Well, if you don't want to poke the fire, you can always poke me with it." She looked at his face and saw his grin.

"Brock..." she began, but he silenced her with a wave of his hand.

"Nope, don't say anything. All if forgiven, if you will forgive me."

"Well, I..." she paused for a moment in thought. "Of course I forgive you Brock."

"Great! I'm glad that's settled! Here now, take this stick! Oh, and, Margie? Don't poke too hard, okay?"

She laughed and let the joy of being happy again cleanse her heart. It felt good to laugh; it felt good to be on good terms with her best friend. And even though they were still stranded on the island, all seemed right with the world.

* * * * * * * * * *

Later that afternoon, a tired, bunch of sunburned children all tramped back to the castle, clean and refreshed from a day of swimming and relaxation. With their bellies full from the fish they had cooked over the bonfire on the beach, they all looked forward to getting to bed early that night. They had spent hours watching the sea, fanning the flames and smoke into the air with large fir branches, hoping that somebody would see their signals. When they seemed to have had enough of the water, sand and smoke, Brock and Margie gathered them all up and walked back up to the castle. As they passed by the orchard, Brock had each of the children gather as much fruit as they could carry and take it inside to the kitchen for breakfast. He stood at the gate of the castle, watching as the last of the group went through the door. Glancing up at the sky, he decided there was enough time left in the day to do one final thing. The skeleton key he had found in the lab was burning a hole in his pocket, and he was eager to find out what was in the locked room. He planned to tell Margie his plans as soon as everyone was inside.

CHAPTER FOURTEEN

The Trap

Nettle was standing behind her favorite tree in the orchard, watching the strangers return from the beach. She was careful not to make her presence known. She was not supposed to be there; the last time she had returned home from visiting the fortress, her father had given her a beating when he found out where she had been, but something drew her to these children. She had told her mother about the Savior and her mother had shushed her telling her to be silent about the strangers.

"They will only bring us evil and not good," she had told her.

Nettle refused to believe it – what evil had they brought to their village, except for more tension and arguing? Now that was not anything new. She yearned to go up to them and talk some more, but as soon as the young man went inside, the gate slowly closed behind him. Her heart sank – she knew what would happen if she was caught out here again. Uncle Bryan and Kato, chained up like animals in the middle of the village were setting the example of what would happen to those who disobeyed the words of Mordecai. Nettle knew

Matthew and Raul were only trying to protect their people, but was what her Uncle and Kato had done really that serious? Matthew had called a meeting of all the villagers, who had come running from all directions. The two accused men were placed in the front of everyone and they all had watched as Matthew chained Kato and Uncle Bryan up in the middle of the village. Their home for the next three days would be the dirt they sat on. Matthew sternly commanded that no one was to talk to the prisoners. At the end of three days, Matthew would reevaluate them and see if they were repentant. Uncle Bryan had such a lump on his head that Nettle wondered if he would even last *that* long. The storm did not help matters any either. Matthew remained hardened to the cries of Mariah and Buttercup. He sent the villagers off to their homes vowing to chain up anybody else who violated his law. Not only had the storm wreaked havoc on their people, but most of their gardens were flattened, and some of their livestock died to overexposure. A few of the thatched roofs blew off their huts sending the devastated occupants fleeing to the nearest hut. It was going to take days to get everything back the way it had been. Nettle did not see why they could not just join the group of children in the fortress. They would be safe enough inside the stone walls.

Just then, the loud thunderous bellow of the 'shell' began its low and mournful moaning sound, meant to scare the children away. Nettle covered her ears at the sound, hoping it would not frighten the children. She glanced up towards the mountain cliff and knowing just where to look, she saw a figure standing back in the bushes. Even from where she sat, she could tell it was her father. Quickly she moved behind the tree, hoping he had not seen her. She could never go home if he had, but where could she run and hide? He knew every spot on the island. That was not saying much because it was not very big, measuring four miles long and one mile wide. It was small enough to be hidden from the enemy, but to Nettle it felt like a prison.

The sound of the 'shell' stopped and Nettle took her hands away from her ears. She remained where she was, not daring to move in case her father decided to look down into the orchard. She did not know how long she would have to sit there, but she knew she could not come out until he left the lookout rock.

* * * * * * * * *

When the sound of the 'shell' had started, Brock had rushed to Margie's side in hopes that he could keep her from panicking and losing her head again. Although she was nervous about the sound, she kept her cool and remained calm for the children. Brock had a feeling it was something the people of the island were doing to scare them, and he reassured everyone that there was nothing to fear.

"Maybe tomorrow we can see if we can find where they live and talk with them. If Nettle speaks English like we do, then most likely they all speak the same language."

Margie was not so sure they would be welcome in their village if they were working so hard to try to scare them away. Nevertheless, she wanted to find someone who could help them get some clothing and maybe give them some food other then fish and fruit.

With everyone gathered together, Brock decided it was a good time to mention his idea of going into the locked room. Some seemed enthusiastic about the idea, but others, like Margie, again doubted that it was a good idea.

"Come on, Marg, I know you're curious to find out what is in there. What could it hurt? If there isn't anything of interest, we will just lock it up and leave it alone."

"I still think it's odd that they left the key after all this time. It's as if they want us to go in there. The way I see it, there is something bad in that room. They try everything to get us to leave, and suddenly they give us a key to the locked room. Something isn't right."

No matter how hard she tried to sway Brock from changing his mind, he would not give up the idea. Finally, giving Brock and her fears over to the Lord, she agreed to go up with him. All eleven children carefully climbed up to the top of the stairs, stopping at the locked door.

Brock dug the key out of his pocket, slipped it into the keyhole and heard a click as he turned it. He waited. Nothing happened, so he lifted the latch. Another loud click echoed through the hallway, and a peculiar humming noise began. Still nothing seemed out of the ordinary; so he opened the door, took the key out of the lock, and stepped into the room. The room contained two large trunks and a small window with bars.

"Come on in, Margie, everything is fine."

Unsure of the humming noise she heard, she paused at the door wondering if it was safe. She felt a small push from behind and heard Tina whisper, "Go ahead and see what's in those trunks!"

Taking a chance, Margie stepped in and walked over to one of the wooden chests. Brock opened it and pulled out a piece of bark. On it were the same symbols he had seen before, but this time the paper said,

You thought there would be treasure, but greed always brings death.

Underneath the paper was a pile of clothing. Maybe gold and silver could bring death because the Bible said that the love of money was the root of all evil, but clothing certainly would not bring death!

Margie gasped in awe as she pulled out the long, flowing robes of regal colors. They may not have come looking for gold treasure, but they had found exactly what they were looking for. A whole chest of clothing; it was an answer to prayer! The Lord was faithful to supply all their need according to His riches in glory!

Tina, Oakley, Larissa, and Aaron had followed them into the room. Mark had been holding the door open, but let go of it so he could keep Kia from entering.

The hard slam of the door shutting startled everyone in the hallway, making Blossom screech. Mark ran over to the door and pulled on the latch but it did not budge.

"Brock, can you open the door from inside?" Mark hollered through the heavy wood.

A muffled voice yelled back, "There's no latch in here! You have to open it from out there!"

Mark tried again but the door refused to open. "I need the key! Can you push it under the door?"

Brock tried, but the skeleton key would not fit underneath. Mark rubbed his forehead, annoyed that he had let go of the door. What was he going to do now?

The humming sound grew louder, and Mark's eyes widened in fear as the whole wall seemed to move away from him. If the wall was moving away from him, then that meant it was closing in on the others inside the room! Mark frantically banged on the door with his fists. "Brock, you have to get out! The wall is closing in on you!"

Margie, Tina, and Larissa were excitedly examining all the regal clothing in the trunks. Oblivious to the danger behind them, they held up each garment trying to picture which child it would fit best. Feeling a hand on her shoulder, Margie looked up. Brock's face was pale as a sheet. She quickly stood up, still holding a purple robe.

"What's wrong, Brock? You're as white as a ghost!"

"I think you were right about this room not being safe." He held the key out in his hand and looked at it as if it were evil. Closing his fist over it, he walked over to the window, and shoved the trunk out from under it. He tried pulling at the metal bars, but they had been welded into the stone. They could chip the stone away, but they did not have the time, or the tools, to chip their way out. He hurried back over to the door.

"Mark! Run outside to the back of the castle, and I will drop the key out to you! Come back and unlock the door once you get it!"

"Brock, what is going on? You still haven't told me what's wrong?" Margie's voice was on the verge of panic again.

Brock pointed to the inside wall of the room. It did not look like anything to her for a few seconds, but as she watched, she noticed the wall seemed to be creeping towards her. She quickly looked back at Brock.

"What is it doing? Am I seeing things?"

Brock shook his head. "If the wall keeps moving and we don't get that door opened, it will crush us."

Overhearing their conversation, Tina let out a whimper of fright. "I don't want to be crushed! Get us out of here!"

Brock was standing at the window waiting for Mark to appear on the ground. He hoped Mark could open the front gate by himself, or at least get Teddy to help him. It seemed to be hours before Mark came running around the corner and stopped under their window. He cupped his hands over his mouth and shouted up, "Okay, I'm ready!"

Brock passed his hand through the bars and held the key over the ground, letting it go as Mark reached up to catch it. He missed, but it did not take long to find the black key in the grass. He gave Brock the thumbs up signal and ran away again.

Brock breathed a sigh of relief. "Once he comes in, he will unlock the door with the key, and we won't have to worry about a thing."

Mark quickly returned to the second floor and called out, "I'm going to unlock the door now!"

The trapped children heard the key rattling in the keyhole, and the latch clattered, but to their dismay, the door did not open.

"It won't work!" Mark's voice was frantic.

Tina whimpered loudly, and Larissa and Oakley joined her crying, adding to the confusion.

"Keep quiet!" hollered Brock on the brink of panic himself, "I can't think with all that noise!" The walls were inching ever so slowly toward them, and Brock did not know how much time they had.

"Margie, throw the clothing out the windows so we can get them later." Brock wanted them to stay busy to help keep their mind off what was happening.

Without any questions, Margie began to toss the clothing out the window, encouraging Tina to help her. Tina was still whimpering, and Margie wondered if there were a chance a cry for help might be heeded. She leaned close to the bars and shouted out loudly, "Help! Help us! Please help us!"

"Who's going to help us?" Brock looked at her if she had lost it again.

"Maybe Nettle will hear us and get help. Maybe the Lord will hear us and send an angel to save us. I don't know, but it's worth a try!" Margie continued tossing the clothes out, all the while shouting out the window.

Oakley tugged on Brock's arm and quietly said to him, "Can we pray for safety? I am scared and only the Lord can help us now."

Brock agreed and had everyone kneel down on the stone floor while he prayed a prayer that the Lord would hear them and get them out of this alive.

* * * * * * * * *

Nettle was still sitting behind the tree in the orchard when she saw the gate open, and a lone figure go racing around the corner and disappear behind the fortress. Within another minute, he had run back and ran over the drawbridge back into the courtyard.

"They must be playing a game," she thought. "It looks fun. I wish I could join in their games."

She peeked around the side of the tree, looking up at the cliff. Her father was gone and there was not any lookout on the rock for the moment. She got up and walked towards the drawbridge. The gate was still open, enough for her small body to go through. She stood on the far side of the draw-bridge, contemplating the idea of crossing over.

All of a sudden, she heard the cries for help. The calls were pleading, as if their very lives were at stake. Nettle's heart stopped. Could they have gone into the locked room? How did they get the key to the door? Without hesitation, Nettle turned around and ran back towards the path that led to her village. She knew that Uncle Bryan and Kato would know what to do. She would have to figure out a way to get them unchained from the block in the center of the village, but she would find a way. The children were in danger, and she was the only one who could help them.

Nettle approached the village and prayed a quick prayer to the God of the strangers.

"Dear God, if you love those children and really are their God, please keep all the villagers away from the path so I can get help. Help me get Uncle Bryan and Kato unchained and keep me from getting in trouble. Amen."

She finished just as she arrived at the village and hurried down the path that led straight through the middle. She passed her own hut quickly, not wanting her father or mother to come out and stop her. Her father would surely lock her up, probably forever, if he even suspected what she was going to do. She walked a few paces to her neighbor's hut and quietly lifted the grass mat covering the front door. She saw Bryan's wife, Buttercup, standing over a small fire with little Tomas crying on the mat next to her on the floor. Buttercup looked tired, and worry lines creased her pretty, young forehead.

Nettle slipped inside and let the mat fall closed behind her. Buttercup turned around to see who had entered her home.

"Nettle," she said softly. Her puffy, red eyes revealed that she had been crying.

Nettle walked over to baby Tomas and picked him up. He instantly stopped crying and laid his head on her shoulder. "I need to talk to you, Aunt Buttercup." She patted Tomas's back and his eyes began to close.

"What is it, Nettle? You look worried."

"You must promise not to tell Matthew or my father about this." She looked into Buttercup's blue eyes, pleading for her help. Buttercup brushed some strands of blonde hair away from her face, tucking them back into the loose bun on the back of her head.

"We need to unchain Uncle Bryan and Kato so they can rescue the children at the fortress."

Buttercup's eyes widened. "You are forbidden to go down there, Nettle. So are Bryan and Kato. They must remain locked up for another night." Her lip quivered as she thought about how much they had suffered already. Bryan had been cold and miserable when she had snuck out to him last night to bring them something to eat. She had rubbed his hands to try to get the circulation going again, but the coughing and sneezing she heard from him made her worry even more.

Nettle walked over to the door and peeked outside. The coast was still clear. She could just make out Bryan and Kato's slumped forms off in the distance. She turned back to Buttercup. "We have got to do something! They're only children! What if it was baby Tomas or me shut up in that room? Somehow, they unlocked the trap door, and they were begging for their very lives! If we don't help them, they are going to be crushed! Uncle Bryan knows his way in the fortress, and I am sure he knows how to stop the wall!" Her voice was frantic. She knew even as they spoke that the wall was still moving, closer by the second. She did not know how much time they had left.

Buttercup looked nervously at Nettle. "But how do we unlock them? Matthew has the only key to their chains. We would be beaten close to death if they found us unlocking them- or if they even knew of our plan."

"But don't you want Uncle Bryan to be unchained? Don't you care about him?"

Buttercup covered her face with her hands and began to sob. "Of course I care, Nettle." She sputtered between her hands. "How could you even ask that?" She suddenly stopped and wiped her eyes. "All right, I will help you. I think I have an idea. Let's hope it works." She explained her idea to Nettle as she took the baby from her. "I will run to Pearlie and Matthew's hut, telling them Tomas is sick. You must follow me and run into their hut and find the key while they are gone. Unlock the men and run as quickly as you can back to the fortress. May you have wings like the eagles; you will need them when Matthew finds the men gone."

Buttercup laid Tomas down on his little bed and closed her eyes as she gave his leg a little pinch. He woke up with a start and started screeching loudly. "Sorry, baby dear," she kissed his fuzzy, little head, "someday you'll understand why I did what I did."

She pushed Nettle out the door and raced off to Matthew's hut. Pearlie was the doctor of the village, but Matthew always liked to go with her during her visits, offering what advice he could give. He liked to be in control of all situations.

Nettle watched as Buttercup ran into their hut, and she heard their excited voices. All three rushed out and went down the path to Buttercup's hut. As Buttercup followed the two inside the hut, she gave Nettle a look that said, "Now!"

Nettle hurried into the vacant hut and looked around the room. Where would he hide the key? The sunlight from the window blinded her for a second. She turned around and saw the light reflecting off something behind the doorway. It was the key!

She grabbed it, ran out of the hut, and hurried down the path to the men. They were sitting in the middle of a circular fence made of vines tied to some sticks stuck in the ground. Covered with mud and grime from the last few days, they sat with their heads hung down in shame. Bryan did not even look up her when she softly called his name.

"Uncle Bryan! I have the key! I am going to free you, but you must come with me." As she stepped over the vines, her feet sunk into the soft mud, the bottom of her dress dragging in the water.

"Kato! Uncle Bryan! Look at me!" she whispered as loud as she could, glancing back at the hut where Matthew and Pearlie were. There was still no sign of anybody to stop her. She knelt in front of Bryan and took his hands in hers. They were so cold. She quickly unlocked his chain and moved to Kato. He looked at her with sad, weary eyes.

"You're going to get into a lot of trouble, Nettle. Don't you care about yourself? They will beat you to an inch of your life!"

She nodded. "I know, Kato. It doesn't matter anyhow. The children at the fortress need your help. They are locked in the 'room!'"

She helped Kato up and looked at Bryan. "Come, Uncle, we must hurry before they see us!"

Bryan wanted to leave more then anything, but he was afraid of what would happen when Matthew and Raul found them gone. He almost refused, but then the same hopeless feeling of despair made him figure it did not matter anyway. He could either stay and die here, or take the opportunity and escape and be free. It certainly was worth the chance.

He slowly stood up, and grimaced as his back screamed in pain. He had sat hunched over for so long that it hurt to stand upright again.

"Hurry!" Nettle grabbed the men's hands and pulled them to the edge of the circle of vines. They stepped over and without another moment's hesitation, she pulled them into the woods before one of the villagers saw them. They were free!

CHAPTER FIFTEEN

A Close Call

Inside their prison, Tina, Margie, Larissa, Oakley, Aaron, and Brock, all formed a line on their knees, and held hands as the wall inched closer to them, leaving them only a four-foot space of life left. Their cries out the window had stopped and now their cries to their heavenly Father lifted up for their very lives!

"Dear God!" Brock prayed, "You could not have sent us to this island to die a senseless death! Please send somebody to rescue us! The circumstances do not look good, but You promised that all things would work together for good, according to Romans 8:28. Please make something good come out of this!"

Hearing pounding on the door, Brock paused in his prayer. "We're still here Mark!" Brock reassured the others on the opposite side of the door. "Keep praying for us!"

Margie began praying where Brock had left off. "Oh, dear Jesus, please save us! Have mercy on us and get us out of this prison! We're sorry for not seeking Your will before coming into this room. Please forgive us, and let us get out of this alive!"

The wall had moved another few inches and was touching the end of Brock's knees. He glanced at Margie with a look of anguish as he stood up. Her heart went out to him, and she wanted to go over to him and give him a big hug, but she could not move from her spot in the row. Tina and Larissa were crowding her, clinging to her with all their might. The drone of the gears pushing the wall was like the incessant buzzing of an annoying mosquito in her ears. One trunk had splintered apart before Brock could move it to one side. The other trunk was set along the back wall where they were kneeling.

A loud commotion outside the door caused everyone to look with renewed hope at the door. Muffled voices drifted through the wall. Someone began pounding on the door again, which was now directly in front of Brock. He called out with hope in his voice, "What's going on out there?"

Mark's voice came through the door, as if he was cupping his mouth against the wood, "Some men are here! They know how to stop the wall!"

Brock and Margie's eyes met. Did they hear Mark right? Another minute passed, which felt like an eternity as the wall pressed even closer. They were all standing now, so they could still have some breathing space. The weight of the wall was oppressive! Margie felt like she was going to suffocate, but then a peace settled over her. She relaxed as Tina and Larissa hid their faces against her tattered dress. How could she feel so calm and brave?

For an instant the buzzing stopped and a silence that hurt their ears filled the room. Then suddenly the humming began again, but this time the children watched with baited breath as the wall slowly began to move in the opposite direction. They all cheered as the realization that they were safe flooded their beings. Brock grabbed Oakley and Aaron in a big hug and began laughing. Margie stood watching him, wondering if he had lost his mind, but his deep laughter was contagious and she broke out into a giggle too. Tina wrapped her arms around Margie's neck and cried in relief. Larissa just stood there unsure of what was happening.

Mark pounded on the door from the outside. "What's going on in there? Is everyone all right?"

Blossom's little squeaky voice piped up, "Argie? You comin' out now? I miss you a lot!"

Margie could not help but smile as she answered the toddler, "I miss you too, Honey. I'll be out soon!"

It seemed like an eternity for the wall to return to its original position, but finally there was a click and it stopped. The buzzing sound ceased and sweet peace and quiet filled the room.

The doorknob rattled and then the door swung open wide. Brock was the first to reach the door. He looked out at all the children waiting breathlessly in the hallway. Their faces were pale and worried. A man whom he did not know peered into the room.

"You can come out now," he said in a deep, raspy voice. "You are safe."

Visibly shaken, Brock stepped through the doorway, feeling as if he were stepping over the threshold of death into life. Behind him came Aaron, Oakley, Larissa, Tina, and Margie. When the other children saw their dear friends alive and well, tears of joy and relief streamed down all their faces.

Scotty stood back as he watched the others hug each other and lift their hands in thanksgiving to their Savior. He felt too embarrassed to join in his friend's rejoicing, and remained in the shadows where they would not notice him.

When the cheering subsided, Brock called his little flock together and said, "We must bow down and thank our Heavenly Father for hearing our cries!"

Nettle, Bryan, and Kato stood off to the side, watching the children express their thankfulness to the God of Heaven.

It was a mystery to them Who this Heavenly Father was that they were talking about, but Bryan felt a stirring in his soul like he had never felt before. These children had a sense of joy and peace that he had been longing for. He glanced at Nettle and saw that she had tears in her eyes. She turned away from him and wiped them away. Bryan put his hand on her shoulder. "You okay?" he asked her.

She looked at him and shrugged. "Why aren't they thanking me for hearing their cries? If it wasn't for me, then they would be dead right now!"

Bryan frowned, unsure what to say. He looked at the kneeling group of children and watched their leader, the young man who had been in the locked room.

As if feeling the weight of Bryan's stare, Brock looked up and met his eyes. Brock stood up and approached him with his hand out. Bryan stepped back, not knowing what Brock was doing.

Brock smiled. "It's called a handshake, something we do when we want to meet somebody else, or even thank them for something. My name is Brock, and I want to thank you for saving our lives. You came at just the right time. A few minutes longer, and, well, I don't even want to think of what might have happened! How did you know we needed help?"

A little overwhelmed by it all, Bryan cleared his throat. He felt so dizzy and confused. His thoughts cleared enough for him to remember Nettle coming to unlock his and Kato's chains. "Nettle came and freed us. I am Bryan. That is Kato." He pointed at the other man standing next to him. Kato nodded in greeting. Nettle stood behind him, looking hurt and forlorn.

Brock knelt down and looked into Nettle's face. "Then I must thank you most of all for going to get these wonderful men. God used you to hear our cries. Without you, we would not be alive right now. You were a vessel used by the Lord."

He reached out and gently patted her shoulder. The look of hurt evaporated from her face as the meaning of his words dawned on her. Their God had used *her* to save them? Awe and wonder filled her eyes. She wanted to know this God of theirs!

"Will you teach me more of your Savior?" she asked timidly.

At Brock's broad grin, she smiled back and felt instantly at ease.

"Of course I will, Nettle. By the way, do you mind if I call you Nellie?"

Surprised, she cocked her head, as if thinking about what he asked. She liked the sound of the name, and it seemed so much nicer then Nettle. She asked quietly, "What does it mean?"

"It means 'bright one.' It suits you much better then Nettle. You are not a thorn at all."

Margie stepped over to Nettle, now Nellie, and smiled. "We already met, but I wanted to say thank you for what you did for us too." She reached her arms out for a hug. Nellie rushed into her embrace and hugged her back.

"My father is so wrong about you," she whispered in Margie's ear. "Will you be my friend?"

"Of course I will." Margie gladly consented.

A loud thump made everyone turn. Bryan had collapsed in a heap on the floor! Brock rushed over to him. "What's wrong with him?" He asked, feeling Bryan's pulse.

Nellie ran over and knelt down next to him. "He was being punished for coming into the fortress a few days ago. He and Kato spent the night outside in the storm."

Margie's eyes grew wide. "That big storm we had just the other day?"

Kato stepped forward, looking pale and sickly himself. "Yes. It was terribly windy and cold. We must lie down and rest, but I am not sure if we should stay here. It is against

Mordecai's writing to come in here. It says the fortress is haunted by King Farrell and anyone who enters will never leave again."

Brock looked into Kato's eyes. Kato did not look much older then himself. "You don't believe that, do you?"

Kato glanced away for a second, then turned back and replied, "No. I have been here before and nothing ever happened. It's just a made-up story to keep all the villagers out."

Brock nodded. "Here, help me carry Bryan downstairs. We can make up some beds for you in one of the rooms we have cleaned up down there."

Kato hesitated as Brock bent down to lift Bryan's shoulders. "Kato?"

Kato's face registered concern.

"It will be okay, Kato. Everything will be fine."

Nodding in agreement, Kato took Bryan's legs, and together they carried him downstairs to one of the empty, but clean, rooms.

Brock called out, "Aaron! Mark! Take the boys and gather up some fresh grass so we can make some beds for these men!"

Margie called Tina and instructed her to get a couple of extra tapestries they had in the girl's room and bring them to her.

The boys quickly rushed down the steps to do as Brock had told them. Mark, Aaron, and the other boys worked fast, gathering up the warm grass in large bunches. When they held as much as their arms could hold, they hurried into the castle and into the room where the men were lying down.

"Oh, good, I see you boys have lots of fresh grass. Margie will make up some beds so Bryan and Kato can rest comfortably."

Margie had the boys pile the grass into two long mounds, and then she spread the tapestries over the piles, making a soft bed for the men. Kato helped Brock move Bryan onto one of the soft beds, and then laid himself down closing his eyes in exhaustion.

CHAPTER SIXTEEN

Sharing God's Goodness

B ryan moaned. Margie went over to where he lay and felt his forehead. He was burning up with fever. She gasped when she noticed the swollen, egg-sized sore just above his forehead.

"The poor man," she whispered. She knew she needed to go and get some water and rags. "We need to bring down his fever and get that wound cleaned up." She looked at Nellie. "Do you know what kind of herbs I can give to help him?"

Nellie nodded, but looked grim. "Matthew and Pearlie are the doctors of the village. They know the best herbs for this, but I can try to find some myself. I can't ask them for their advice because they would refuse to help Uncle Bryan. He disobeyed their orders. In fact, *I* can't even go back. My father will beat me again."

Margie put her hand on Nellie's shoulder. "Maybe if I went with you and told him what happened? Maybe he will understand then?"

"Oh, no! He would surely kill you if went near the village. He is convinced you are from Bone's tribe of bandits wanting to steal the treasure."

Surprised, Margie had to laugh a little at the thought. Did she and all the children look like a bunch of bandits? She chuckled, not able to help herself.

Nellie looked a little miffed. "Well, that is what *he* thinks. I never believed it, but he believes what he wants. He is the leader you know. What he says goes."

"I'm sorry," mumbled Margie. "I didn't mean anything by it. It just seemed funny that a bunch of children might be dangerous. How long has it been since you've seen visitors here?"

"Never. I am ten years old, and I have never seen anybody on this island but us. There have never been any visitors to this island for at least sixty years since Bones came and attacked the fortress."

The boys were listening intently. "Was there a big battle?" Mark asked.

"How come you don't live in the castle now?" Scotty asked.

"How many people are left?" Teddy added.

Margie could see that all their questions were overwhelming Nellie, and she hurried between them. Glancing at Brock she commented, "We need to get Bryan and Kato cleaned up and fed. I'll go boil some water and take the smaller children with me. Can we discuss this later?"

Brock looked up and nodded. "Of course; I was getting into the story myself and got distracted."

As Margie walked by Kato, she glanced at his face. "He looks so young," she whispered.

Nellie told her, "He just married my sister a week ago. He has lived on the island for seventeen years."

"Seventeen," mumbled Margie. "He's only three years older then me."

Bryan moaned again. She had to move quickly. "Brock, stay here with them, and I will take the others out. Do you need anyone else to stay and help?"

"Let Tina and Aaron stay with me. They can help if I need it."

"All right then. I will be back as soon as I can." She stood up and called the children. "Come children! We must hurry!" She stopped long enough to pick up Blossom, place her on her hip, and head out into the courtyard, where she instructed the older children to watch the little ones while she gathered up the supplies she needed.

Margie quickly stoked the fire and set a pot of water to boil over the top. When one of the children handed her an article of clothing, she began to rip it into pieces to use for a cool cloth on Bryan's forehead. Nellie had gone outside to hunt down some herbs she could use for the sick man and returned with a handful of Hops flowers and Comfrey leaves. She set the flowers down inside a bowl and poured some boiling water over it.

"Let this sit for a few minutes, and it will help bring his fever down. It will also help take away some of the pain he may be feeling. I will make a poultice with these leaves, and we will cover the sore with it." Together they worked quickly, and soon they were back inside the room where the sick men were.

Brock looked very relieved to see Margie return, and he quickly left Nellie and Margie to work on Bryan. Kato was sleeping peacefully on his little bed, exhausted from the events of the last few days.

Margie dipped her cloth into the pail of water and squeezed it out. Leaning over the sick man, she wiped his forehead and face, hoping to cool his burning head. Nellie knelt close by her side with a worried look on her face.

"Matthew and Pearlie would know just what to do to help him." she commented, glancing at Margie. "They would know what other herbs to use."

Margie smiled at the girl. "I am sure they would," she agreed. She looked over at Kato who was still sleeping soundly on his little bed. "But I think we should also pray and ask the Lord to help them get better too. My God is a God of miracles, and He healed many sick people when He walked on the earth. Would you let me pray for your Uncle, Nellie?"

Nellie looked at Margie with large, brown eyes. "That would be nice. I—I wanted to ask you, but I wasn't sure how." She turned away so Margie would not see her tears.

"Don't ever be afraid of asking the Lord for His help. He knows your heart, sweet child." At Nellie's smile, Margie smiled back and reached for her hand. "You know, it says in the Bible, in Matthew 18:8, that where ever there are two or more gathered in His name, Jesus will be in the midst of them."

"You mean Matthew's name is in the Bible?" Nellie looked shocked.

"Oh, yes, there is a whole book named after him. He was one of Jesus' disciples."

"What is a disciple?"

"A disciple is a follower of Jesus Christ."

"You must be a disciple then too!"

"Well, I guess I am in a way," Margie smiled at the thought. "Now let's pray."

Together they bowed their heads as Margie prayed. She thanked the Lord for His safety during the day and for His goodness in all that He had blessed them with. Then she prayed that the Lord would lay His hand on Bryan and heal him from this sickness. She wanted so much for Nellie and the others to see God's power and see how much they needed Him in their lives. She hoped this would be the chance for them to see a miracle.

When Margie finished, Nellie continued to hold tightly to Margie's hand. The room was so peaceful; it was a feeling that Nellie had not felt in a long time. She kept her eyes closed not knowing what to expect when she opened them.

Would Uncle Bryan be better? She listened and noticed there *had* been a change in his breathing. She opened her eyes. Her uncle looked the same to her, but he was not making the same moaning sounds. She looked at Margie who was feeling his forehead.

"What is it?"

"I think his fever broke. He seems cooler."

Footsteps echoed down the hall, and Brock appeared around the corner with their dinner.

"How is he?" Brock asked as he stepped into the room.

"We prayed for him and as soon as we were done, his fever broke," Margie commented.

Brock looked thrilled. "Praise God!" he said. "We must never forget to thank Him for all the good things He has done for us. It always amazes me how much He loves and cares for us!"

He handed the girls each a bowl of warm broth. Little chunks of meat were floating in the soup, with carrots and beans. Margie looked questioningly at Brock.

"Where did you get the meat?"

"Mark and Aaron went out hunting for something more filling than fruit. They caught a pheasant in a trap they made, and I made soup to stretch it out more. It tastes really good too."

Margie tried a bite and savored the taste of the meat in her mouth. "If I had known you could cook, I would have invited you into the kitchen a long time ago!" she joked.

Kato stirred at the sound of their voices and sat up.

"Looks like I better go and get another bowl of soup," Brock commented. "I will be right back."

Margie watched him leave and suddenly felt tired and worn out. The day seemed to be an endless one with one thing happening after another. How long had it been since she had slept in that morning? God had known she would need that extra hour of sleep. She looked up and saw Kato watching her.

"Are you okay?" he asked her.

"I am completely worn out. I can't wait to go to bed and rest my aching head."

"You must go and lie down then. Nettle and I will stay with Bryan." Kato approached them and laid his hand on Bryan's head. "You did well. He is resting peacefully now. He will be just fine."

Margie's eyes filled with tears from exhaustion. "It wasn't me Kato; it was the Lord. Nothing happens unless it is His will for it to be so."

Kato glanced at her in the flickering candlelight and nodded. "You are very dedicated to your God."

"I owe everything to Him. Without Him I would be lost and on the road to hell."

"You will have to tell me more about Him later. You go rest now. Do not worry about things here."

Margie stood up to leave, but paused before going out the door. She looked back at Kato and said, "Can I ask you something?"

"Yes, of course."

"When we were stuck in that room upstairs, how did you stop the wall from crushing us?"

"There is a little space underneath the staircase in the entryway. A secret panel is on the wall inside with a lever hidden behind it. The lever controls a motor, which connects to the wall upstairs. We pulled the switch and that shut the motor off."

"So that is what that cubby hole is for. We were wondering what the purpose was, other than hiding Coal."

Brock returned with another bowl of soup and handed it to Kato. After saying goodnight to their guests, Brock walked with Margie down the hall and stopped at his door.

"Goodnight Margie. Get a good night's rest. We don't know what tomorrow may hold."

She nodded, and said goodnight as she continued to her door. Little did they know that Brock was right – tomorrow would bring something else that would really test their faith and trust in their Lord.

CHAPTER SEVENTEEN

The Jellyfish

The tall sail hung limp in the still air as the ship sat dead in the water. The previous day's storm had been a rough one at sea, and the stillness of the afternoon came as a welcome relief to the sailors. Without any wind to sail, they sat lounging around the decks laughing and singing.

A man high up in the crow's nest leaned back with his spyglass and surveyed his surroundings. The open sea seemed to stretch on endlessly before him with no sign of land anywhere. He grunted as he lowered his telescope. Would his search never end? Would he ever find what he was looking for? Pulling out a paper from his back pocket, he studied the grids and lines that crisscrossed over the map of the sea. He had marked the spot where he had calculated the island should be, and looked closely at it again. Had he miscalculated the numbers? He scanned the numbers written on the edge of the map and added them up again. As he suspected, the original figure he had come up with was wrong. Grunting again, he pulled out a fountain pen from his shirt pocket and crossed off the first 'X'. He made a second notation a few centimeters from the original mark and looked up. That would make the island another mile or two south of them. Picking up his spyglass again, he scanned the horizon for any sign of land. A bit of haze caught his attention in the otherwise cloudless, bright blue sky. A smoky fog was drifting about a mile or two away. A little breeze began to stir, and the mast began to tremble.

"Yes!" the man whispered to nobody in particular, "Blow, wind, blow!" He waited anxiously as the wind began to pick up. Then suddenly the mast puffed out, and the boat began to move. Putting his spyglass to his eye once again, the man looked out towards the haze. The wind was blowing it away. Through a clearing, he saw what he had been looking for.

"Land ho!" he called excitedly.

* * * * * * * * *

Back at the castle, Scotty looked around and saw that the coast was clear. He ran over to the guard's house and quickly went in, shutting the door behind him. Getting on his knees, Scotty quickly shoved the bedside table over and dug at the loose stones. When his fingers touched the leather pouch, he pulled it out and blew the dust off. He quickly hid the pouch in his torn, dirty shirt close to his skin. He stood up and carefully pulled the table back over the hole. He knew exactly where he was going to hide the pouch from the others, so nobody but he could claim the treasure.

* * * * * * * * *

Brock was busy building a fire in the kitchen that afternoon when Mark came running in. "Hey, Brock, shouldn't we go check to see if there are any ships passing by?"

Brock looked up from where he was kneeling by the fireplace. "Yes, that would be a good idea. Why don't you go to the lookout rock with Aaron and Teddy and see what's out there. Any passing ships should have noticed yesterday's bonfire if they were in the area. Run back as fast as you can if you see anything."

"Okay," Mark said as he headed out the door to find his friends.

A few minutes later the three boys entered the courtyard and found Scotty out near the guardhouse door.

"What are you doing out here?" Aaron asked him.

Scotty looked around and spotted the water pump. "I was just coming out for a drink of water," he muttered to them.

"You look kind of guilty to me," stated Mark. "You better get inside and see if Brock has anything for you to do. We are on a mission so we have to run. See ya!"

Scotty watched them go with a sinking heart. How come Brock never chose him to go on any missions? It was always the bigger boys, though Teddy always seemed to get to go along too.

When the boys were gone, he decided now was the best time to hide his map. He figured the longer he held onto it, the more chance there was of someone else finding it, someone like Brock. Then he would never get his treasure! Scotty ran out of the courtyard and over the drawbridge. Glancing back over his shoulder, he saw that the coast was clear. Nobody had seen him go. He entered the woods near the orchard and searched for a good place to hide his little pouch. He noticed two trees that had grown into one, crisscrossing over each other like an 'X.'

"'X' marks the spot!" Scotty said excitedly. "This is where I will hide my map." He squatted down beside the two trees and dug a little hole underneath the 'X'. Carefully he pulled out his precious map and laid it down in the opening and spread some dirt over it. He looked around for a good-sized stone to cover the gap and found one not too far away. He set it over the hole and stepped back. Nobody would ever find his map now!

* * * * * * * * *

The three ship seekers hurried down the trail and up the side of a mountain that faced the seaside. A large, flat rock sat at the top – Brock had discovered it one afternoon when he had been out exploring the island. It was the perfect spot to watch for ships because they could see all four corners of the ocean. Every afternoon someone had gone out to the rock to check for any ships going past. In the month's time of being on the island, they had seen nothing but whales and dolphins.

The boys reached the top of the mountain and scanned the horizon for any signs of life. Teddy noticed it first.

"Look, guys! I see something!"

"Where?" Mark looked out to where Teddy's finger was pointing. There, not too far from the shore, was a large ship. Small lifeboats were in the water heading towards the beach. An excitement began to well up in the middle of the boys' stomachs until it burst out into whoops of joy. It *had* to be Mr. Carver coming to rescue them!

Mark turned towards Teddy. "Go and tell Brock about the ship. Aaron and I will go down and show our guests where we are staying."

Teddy nodded and ran off as fast as his little legs could carry him. He could not wait to announce the good news to Brock and the others!

* * * * * * * * *

Brock was lying under the water pump in the court-yard trying to get a rock out that Blossom had stuck inside. Peering into the nozzle, he reached in and worked at the large rock that was wedged in the pipe. Mumbling under his breath about curious children touching things they shouldn't, he barely noticed the eager, lively body that came bouncing into the courtyard. It was only when Teddy began tumbling over his words as he jumped around that Brock sat up and looked at him intently.

"Slow down, Teddy! What's going on?"

"A ship! We saw a ship and some people were rowing to the island! Mark and Aaron went down to the beach to meet them."

"You really saw a ship?" Brock looked delighted. "So the fire worked after all! We've been found!" He wiped his hands on the front of his pants and bounded into the castle.

"Margie! Margie! Come quick!"

Margie rushed out of the sick men's room with a frightened look on her face. "What is it, Brock?"

"The boys spotted a ship! A ship, Margie!" He gave a joyful shout and danced a little jig around the hallway.

"Is it Mr. Carver?" she asked, still looking unsure of the news.

"We think so. We will soon find out. Quickly, everyone, let's go gather near the gate and wait for them to arrive."

They all grouped together outside and waited for what seemed like hours. Would they ever get here? Brock peered out over the drawbridge, watching the path that led down to the beach. A gust of wind blew up and the wild howl, so well known to them by now, echoed through the woods raising the hair on the back of Brock's neck. He noticed some shadows coming up the trail and a chill went down his spine. Something was not right, but he could not put his finger on what was wrong. The men came into full view, and Brock stepped back in panic. Mark and Aaron were in front of the men and their faces were pale and fearful. Brock scanned the men's faces for Mr. Carver's gentle one, but he was not there. Another shiver went down his back, his hair bristling again as Mark and Aaron stopped in front of him. They gave him an apologetic look, as if they thought it was their fault, and ran behind Brock into the stunned group of children.

Brock cleared his throat and stood up straight. He was going to make the best of this situation, with the Lord's help.

"Welcome men! I am Brock, leader of the orphans here. Whom do I have the pleasure of meeting?"

One of the men stepped forward and he sure was a frightening sight to behold. He was a large, burly man with jet-black hair tied back in a ponytail, and a neatly trimmed beard that came to a point at the tip of his chin. His big, bushy eyebrows were frowning and his eyes were wide and glaring. A big gold chain hung on his neck and a large, hoop earring stuck out of his ear.

"I am Bruno, Captain of the *Jellyfish*. These are just some of my men; the rest are waiting on the ship for us to return. This here is McAllister, my right hand man."

Another man stepped forward who had a kind looking face, unlike Bruno's rough one. His hair was red, and he had a neatly trimmed beard. Brock noticed a look in his eyes that seemed to say he was lost and looking for something.

McAllister nodded and as he looked over the group of children, his eyes stopped on Scotty's head of bright, red hair. His eyes met Scotty's, and they seemed to lock for a minute before McAllister stepped back behind Bruno again.

"Are you the only ones here?" Bruno asked glancing behind Brock.

"Just me and this group of orphans," he motioned with his hand, and the children came up closer behind him. "Say hello to our guests everyone."

Margie held Blossom tighter to her as she looked at these strangers. She did not trust them. "Hello," she said quietly.

"Well, hello, little lady," Bruno said approaching Margie with a look she did not like. "You sure are a beautiful thing to see after being on the sea for months." He looked at Brock with his bushy eyebrows raised. "Does she belong to you?"

Brock did not like the question or the looks that Bruno was giving Margie. All different kinds of emotions swelled up inside him – he wanted to protect her from these evil looking men, but he did not want to cause trouble either. Standing up taller, he answered them, "She is one of God's children."

Bruno grunted and stepped back again. Margie sighed in relief. Bruno grinned, clearly enjoying his power. He gave Brock another glare. "Is it just children here? What is this place anyway, an orphanage?" he asked again.

"Yes," Brock answered, "eleven children, plus two sick men who are inside the castle."

"Sick? Is it something catching?"

Something told Brock not to go into detail about Bryan and Kato. He gave Bruno as little information as he needed. "No, they have nothing contagious. They will be fine in a day or so."

Margie's heart fluttered wildly as she stared at this sinister looking group of men. The big one frightened her the most, but she prayed a quick prayer asking the Lord to calm her spirit so she would not scare the children with her own fear. An idea suddenly popped into her head, and she bravely stepped forward next to Brock.

"You must all be hungry! Let us fix you something to fill your empty stomachs." Margie knew the way to a man's heart! "It isn't much, but it is good and filling."

Turning around to the children, she said, "All you children eight years and older go and gather as much food as you can. We have guests, and we need to be hospitable and show them some kindness." She waved them away with her free hand. "Go on now!"

Brock was stunned at her calm and controlled demeanor. His heart swelled with pride. Everyone sprang into action, some going out over the drawbridge to the orchards and gardens, while the visitors entered through the massive gate and into the courtyard.

Bruno and his men were very interested in looking around the castle grounds, and without hesitation, they began combing every inch of ground and wall. Brock wondered what they were looking for. It did not seem as if they were just interested in the archeological construction of the castle itself but something much more serious.

Brock stayed outside to keep an eye on their visitors while Margie went in to tell Bryan and Kato about the men. When she reached their room, she saw Nellie had already told them. Kato looked at Margie, and she saw fear in his eyes.

"You let them in?" he demanded from where he sat on his bed.

"What do you mean? Why shouldn't we have let them in?" She looked bewildered. "Why? Who are they?"

Bryan's face flushed as he struggled to sit up too. "They said they are from the *Jellyfish*. Mordecai warned us about keeping watch for the Jellyfish because they were a mean and wicked group of men; and to think that you let them inside the fortress!"

"But how were we to know? I never read any writings of Mordecai. The only Mordecai I know of is the name on the door down in the cavern!" Margie felt close to tears. What had they done?

CHAPTER EIGHTEEN

Treasure Seekers

"Don't like 'dem," whispered Blossom from the corner she was sitting in with some of the other children. Larissa turned to her and put her finger to her lips as she tried to hush the little girl.

"They 'mell yucky!" She closed her eyes and stuck out her tongue. Some of the other children chuckled, but Larissa looked mortified.

"Blossom, don't say that! They might be able to help us get away from this island!" Larissa looked around for Margie, hoping she might be able to help, but saw that she was busy keeping the men's mugs filled with fresh, cold water. She watched Margie wipe some sweat away from her forehead and felt sorry for her. The men were loud, and she did have to admit that they did not smell very good, though she was not sure if the orphans themselves smelled very good either. It was not as if *they* had a bath every day! Neither did she like the way the men were gawking at Margie and Tina, who was also helping serve. She glanced around hoping that Brock was nearby keeping an eye on the girls. She had an uneasy feeling about the strangers and did not want anything to happen to their orphan's little group.

Just then, Brock entered the dining room with a large platter of fresh fruit and vegetables. He set it on the table in front of the men who eagerly reached forward and grabbed at the food. Not able to watch the men eat so sloppily, Larissa turned away in disgust. She wondered if all sailors were without manners. She tried to remember if that was how Mr. Carver's sailors ate on the *Haven*, but realized they had never eaten around the children.

Brock stepped back and glanced at Margie, who looked hot and tired from all her work. The men had been eating for the last half an hour and they did not seem like they were ever going to stop. He did not like the attention they were giving Margie and Tina and decided to keep a close watch on the men. He did not trust them. He stepped over towards the table, and Bruno glanced up at him.

"How long have you been here, Boy?" Bruno asked Brock.

"We've been here about a month. We were on our way to Florida when there was a fire on our ship. Mr. Carver, the missionary who was taking us, sent us out in a lifeboat just in case they could not put the fire out. The line that connected us snapped during the night, and we drifted away."

"This Mr. Carver: you said he was a missionary? Like a preacher man?"

"Yes, sir-," Brock stopped when Bruno interrupted him with a loud laugh.

"Sir! He called me sir! Ha! When did I ever gain that honor? If that don't beat all!" He sat back on the bench and slapped his knee.

McAllister, who was sitting next to him, frowned and whispered something to Bruno. Bruno grunted in reply and motioned to Brock as he took a drink from his cup. "I should send someone to get the rum from the ship. That would taste a whole lot better then this flavorless junk! Go ahead and finish your story, Boy."

Brock cleared his throat and continued. "We met Mr. Carver in the orphanage in Boston. He kept coming back over the course of a year, and during that time we all started listening to his words, and he gained our trust. He taught us about Jesus and how He died on the cross for us to save us from our sins."

Bruno again interrupted Brock. "What sins could you have committed? You are barely out of diapers! All of you put together probably haven't even committed half of what I have done."

Margie stepped forward with some more water to refill their glasses. "Then *you* might want to hear what our Jesus has done. He came to redeem us all from our sins."

Bruno's eyes darted to Margie's flushed, sweaty face. "Ah, the little lass can speak. What beautiful eyes you have, my sweet lady." He reached out and took Margie's arm.

Brock's brow furrowed, and he quietly commanded Margie, "Go out and make sure the boys are gathering more fruit. We can't have them sitting on the job now, can we?"

Margie pulled her arm away from Bruno, and without another word rushed into the hall and out the castle door.

"She's your gal, isn't she? I can tell by the way you look at her. You're a lucky man, Boy. She's a right pretty gal, she is. But what about the other little lass over there?" Bruno scrutinized Tina as she bustled around the table.

Brock tried to stand as tall as he could. He calmly and bravely answered, "We are all Christians here, and we are going to conduct ourselves wisely among the children, and children they are, Sir. That is all they are."

Bruno stared at Brock, wondering if he should stare him down and show him who was really the boss here, but decided to let it go. He had more important things to attend to right now. He looked away and slapped the table with his hand. "Okay, Men, time to get moving and search this old castle. We need to find what we came for and then move on out." With one last drink, Bruno stood up. "Have you searched this castle from stem to stern?" he asked Brock.

"We have explored some, but we have never found anything worth getting excited about."

"We'll see about that," Bruno grunted as he stood up and made his way over to the door. "Men, search the downstairs rooms, walls, floors and ceilings. Look for anything that might be a secret door." The others all stood up and filed out the door behind Bruno.

Brock watched as the men tramped all through the castle foyer, examining every crevice and nook. He had no idea what they might be looking for, unless there was some hidden treasure buried somewhere in the castle. He went into the room where Kato and Bryan were recuperating and shut the door behind him. "Kato, how are you doing?"

Kato looked warily at Brock and motioned him to come closer. "You must not trust those men. Margie told me about them, and they are here to cause trouble. You must get them to leave."

"I can't! They're searching the castle for something."

Kato's face paled. "You must gather the children together and protect them. Those men are going to be angry if they don't find what they are looking for."

"Do you know what it is?"

Kato shrugged. "It could be anything, but with men like these they usually are seeking treasure and ill gotten gain. Gather the children up and send them into our room."

Brock quickly left to collect the children, but as he headed down the hall, he noticed Bruno going up the stairs. He watched him start for the door of the trap-room. Panic rose up in his stomach, and he bounded up the stairs two at a time. "Bruno! Don't go in there!"

Bruno paused; his hand was still in mid-air as he was reaching for the doorknob. "What? Did you just say '*Don't go in there?*' Why? Is there something you are hiding from me?"

"No, of course not," Brock answered.

"But you don't want me to go into this room, correct?" Bruno demanded.

Brock pointed to the door. "That's right. It's a trap. The walls will close in on you and crush you."

It was then that Brock noticed there were a few other sailors from the *Jellyfish* exploring the second floor. They all had stopped and were watching Brock carefully.

"Really! And why would you care about me anyway?"

"Because you aren't ready to die – you haven't repented of your sins and received Jesus into your heart yet."

Bruno snorted. "Is that all you can think about? Look boy, when I was a wee lad, my mother went to church, and I heard all those Bible stories. They never did me any bit of good. God is a just a kid's fairy tale. He's not real and does not work miracles. If He was real I would have found my treasure long ago."

"Perhaps you are looking for the wrong treasure," Brock commented. "The pearl of great price is what the Lord can offer His children. Eternal life and the glory of heaven; being with the Lord face to face is all the treasure I need."

"Well, good then. You won't mind if I go in here and take this other treasure that you won't need." Bruno opened the door and disappeared into the room. The door slammed behind him.

Brock waited, but there was no sound of gears starting up or of the wall beginning to move. The door swung opened and Bruno angrily rushed out. He ran over to Brock and grabbed him by the shoulders.

"You took it! The chest is empty! You stole my treasure! You were trying to trick me with that preaching trash!" He shook Brock and screamed, "Where is it! Where'd ya hide the gold?"

Brock tried to answer, but Bruno was shaking him too much. His teeth rattled and his head pounded as he tried to pull away from Bruno's vise-like grip.

McAllister, who had just started up the stairs, took the steps two at a time. When he reached the top he shouted, "Stop it, Bruno! You're going to kill the boy!"

Bruno let go as suddenly as he had taken hold and stepped back. Brock stumbled back but caught himself just in time. He put his hand up to his head and gasped for breath. "I-I-I n-n-never found any gold."

Bruno's hand went up as if to strike Brock's face, but McAllister stepped in between them. "It won't do any good to strike him, Bruno. Let him explain first."

Between gritted teeth, Bruno called his men over to him. "Lock this boy up in the room downstairs with those sick men. Get all the children together and lock them up too. If they won't tell us where the gold is, then we will force them to talk. They won't eat or drink until we get what we came for!"

McAllister gently took Brock's arm and helped him down the stairs and into the room where Kato and Bryan were.

"Thank you," Brock muttered as he sat down next to Kato. Then glancing up he asked McAllister, "Why are you being so nice? How did you get stuck working with such a cold-hearted man?"

McAllister looked away for a minute. "I made some wrong choices in my life, and I don't wish to see you or any of these boys and girls make the same mistakes. However, Bruno is my Captain, and though I may not agree with all he does, I still have to obey his orders. Your God sounds like a wonderful leader, and I respect the fact that you want to obey the best leader in the world. Someday I would like to get to know Him, but for now I have to live with my bad decisions." He quickly left the room and began helping the other men gather up the children.

When all eleven orphans were in the room, Bruno stood at the door and said, "When you decide to tell me where the treasure is, then you will go free. However, that will only be when we actually find the treasure. You will all die and rot here if you refuse to tell me. We are going to keep searching every inch of this castle, and believe me, we will find what we are looking for. We *will* find it!"

He stormed out of the room and slammed the door behind him. There was some scuffling on the other side of the door, and then a muffled voice said, "I have guards here watching so nobody better try to escape!" and with that, he was gone.

CHAPTER NINETEEN

The Story of Mordecai's Castle

"We're in for it now," announced Bryan from his corner of the room.

Margie glanced up from where she was sitting with her back against the cold stonewall next to the door. Blossom was sitting on her lap, and the other girls were crowded against her, nervously looking around, wondering what was going to happen to them.

"What do you mean?" Margie asked quietly, unsure if she wanted to hear Bryan's answer.

Bryan sat up and got as comfortable as he could on the thin bed. "Well, I am sure Bruno and his men are quite serious; they will not let us out of this one very easily."

The children all looked around at each other in fear as Bryan continued, "Since we have nothing better to do, I might as well tell you the story about this fortress." He cleared his throat and began weaving a story of intrigue that left them breathless.

"About seventy years ago, a captain name Jack Farrell sailed from New England, looking to start a new life. He docked his boat in the New York harbor and moved his very

179

pregnant wife into an apartment in the city. City life was not what he had imagined it to be, and the cold of the winter did nothing to help. They lived in the slums, with rats and roaches running freely through the holes in the walls. His wife and newborn son caught influenza and died shortly after. There was nothing left for him. He did not know where he was going, but found a group of sorry, life-worn sailors and used what money he had left to hire them to sail his ship. This group of men set sail and disappeared for many years. During that time, he discovered this island, and to the tired, heartbroken man, it seemed like paradise. He and his men explored the land for days, checking it out for natives, or for any proof that somebody owned it. Finding it unoccupied, Jack and his sailors began to build this fortress in the mountains. Protected by the giant cliffs surrounding them, they made plans to drill into the mountainside and make a hideout for themselves should they ever need it.

He eventually sailed back to America to collect a few supplies, livestock, and seeds to start his own farm and gardens; however, most of this fortress was built by materials he found here on the island."

Brock nodded, knowing Bryan meant the phosphorescent lighted rocks and other interesting things that made up the castle.

Bryan continued, "He invited some women to come and be wives for the sailors, and they started a little colony. Jack Farrell was their leader, and soon they were calling him King Farrell, because he lived and ruled from the fortress. His new wife Lily was quite content as his new queen. They lived a good life, quietly tending their little gardens and building up the trees they had planted in the orchards.

They began drilling inside the mountains, and it did not take them long to discover the inside to be filled with gold and diamonds, much more then they had ever seen before. They began to mine for it, and then found hiding places for their treasure, not wanting word to get around that they had struck it rich.

King Farrell's fears came true though, when word leaked out during a trip back to New England by a loud-mouthed, boasting sailor. After ten years of living on the island peacefully, a man name Jared Bones, the captain of a group of bandits, sailed in on a ship called the *Jellyfish*. He came and demanded that King Farrell tell him where all the riches were hidden. Of course, King Farrell refused to inform him of his hiding place, so Jared Bones raided the castle and started slaying the men, one by one. He vowed he would not stop until they told him where the treasure was hidden. The women and children, and a few men, escaped into the mountains where they took refuge for days in the gold mines. King Farrell tried to get to the mountain so he could hide too, but Bones found him sneaking off and swiftly took his life. That was where Mordecai, who was King Farrell's best friend and advisor, found them. Bones stood over King Farrell, sword in his hand, with an evil grin on his face.

Mordecai shouted, "Nobody takes the life of a king and lives!" and rushed forward and they fought together, blade upon blade. Mordecai fell when Bones struck him in the side, and Bones left him for dead. Mordecai awoke from unconsciousness and dragged himself up the third flight of stairs. He painstakingly made his way into the secret chamber, which led to the women and children's hideout. He collapsed and did not wake for days.

When he finally came out of his slumber, his mind was never the same again. He began writing page after page of new laws, and required all the people to follow them. Matthew, the leader of our village now, was three years old at the time of the raid. He is the only one who remembers that horrible day."

"So what happened to Bones and his group?" Mark asked.

"The bandits searched for days, and found nothing. They finally left, swearing they would come back one day and find the treasure. We have been watching all these years, waiting for Bones to return. These men are not our friends. They have the sting of death in their hands."

Scotty stood up and paced back and forth, upsetting the other children who were trying to keep from getting their toes stepped on.

"Scotty, sit down please." Margie told him. "There isn't much room for pacing."

Scotty glared at her, and his defiant look surprised her. Brock saw the look too, and in a stern voice commanded, "Scotty, sit down! You must never defy Margie or me, or any adult, you understand?"

Scotty's face turned red and he clenched his fists. "I don't have to listen to you!" He hollered. "I should not even be here! I am not an orphan, and you are not my father!"

He ran to the door and began banging on it, crying hysterically. Brock rushed over and tried to pull him away from the door. Scotty swung his fist and socked Brock right in the eye.

Margie hurried over too and said gently, "Here, Brock, let me try." Turning to the angry boy, she touched his shoulder and said, "Scotty, won't you come and sit down next to me? Can't we talk this over?"

Scotty turned to her and said with gritted teeth, "Nothing you will say can make me stop. I am leaving!"

Unsure of what he meant, Margie backed away and glanced at Brock for help. He just stood there, nursing his sore eye with one hand.

Suddenly the door burst open and Bruno's massive form stepped through the door, knocking Scotty off balance.

"What is going on here?" he demanded. He looked down at the sobbing boy who was now sitting on the floor.

"What are you crying about?" he grumbled. "A big boy like you should not cry!" Bruno reached down and yanked Scotty up onto his feet.

Swallowing back his tears, Scotty stood tall and straight, and looked Bruno in the eye.

"I know where the map is," he said.

"*You* know?" Bruno asked, shocked.

"What?" Margie and Brock echoed beside him.

"I know where the map is that will help find the treasure." Scotty looked boldly at Brock and Margie, for once glad he had made them speechless. He would show them! He would leave and not have to listen to their unfair demands all the time.

"Where is it?" Bruno asked, suspiciously.

"Let me out, and I will show you where it is." Scotty was willing to work out a deal with this big man.

"You promise this isn't a trick just to get away?"

Scotty nodded, "I promise!"

"Because if it is, then you will become my prisoner on my ship, and I will sell you as a slave."

Scotty's face paled, but he nodded in agreement. "I said I promise, and I will keep my promise."

"Okay then, come with me." Grasping the boy behind the neck, Bruno led Scotty out and the door closed behind them.

Margie looked at Bryan in astonishment. "Does he really know where the map is?"

Bryan shrugged. "It could be a trick, but Mordecai also wrote that there was a map hidden somewhere in the fortress, though we never found it. After Bones and his gang left, Mordecai hid the gold in another spot, removed all he could from the castle, and then condemned it. He claimed that King Farrell's body haunted the place and would strike down anyone who dared enter. He came up with the idea of the "trap room" to punish any treasure seekers should they ever return."

Brock interjected a question at this point of the story. "Speaking of that room, how come it did not work when Bruno went back in there?"

"When we turned it off to save your lives, we kept it off so none of the other children would be in danger."

"I see. Margie said the switch is under the stairs, right?"

"Yes, that is correct." Bryan continued, "Mordecai also came up with the idea of making a sound so eerie and frightening that he hoped it would scare off anybody who would dare venture as far as the fortress. He collected large conch shells and some bones, and strung them up along the roof of a cave. When the wind blew, it whistled through the shells and bones, making the eeriest sound you ever heard. He also kept a few larger shells on our lookout rock up above the fortress, and we use it to warn the others back in the village. We call it the "blowing of the shell.""

"So that was what all those sounds were! We were afraid something would come and eat us alive!" Margie remarked. "I am so glad you told us because now we can rest in peace."

"A lot of good it did to scare you all," Kato spoke for the first time.

"We had no where else to go!" Aaron commented as he stretched his legs. "It isn't like we could have just jumped back on our ship and sailed away."

"I wish," muttered Teddy. "When are we are going to be able to leave this room? I'm thirsty, and I need to go to the bathroom."

Trying to take the children's minds off their present situation, Bryan continued his story.

"For a little over sixty years, we have been waiting for the *Jellyfish* to return. No ship ever passed by, and slowly our little clan dwindled; not many men were left alive after the raid. Queen Lily was pregnant at the time of the raid and four months later, she delivered a baby she named Pearlie. Matthew married Pearlie when he was only sixteen and Pearlie was thirteen. They have been our leaders ever since, making sure we live by Mordecai's laws, severely punishing anyone who doesn't."

The room was silent when Bryan stopped talking. Everyone was thinking about what Bryan had told them and wondering if Scotty was okay.

Margie was the one who brought up all their concerns. "Do you think Scotty will be all right with those men?"

Bryan looked at her and slowly shook his head. "Your guess is as good as mine, but if he truly knows where the map is hidden, Bruno is going to be very disappointed. The gold that the map led to was what Mordecai took and hid somewhere else. They won't find any trace of treasure in the caves anymore."

CHAPTER TWENTY

A Peculiar Treasure

Now therefore, if ye will obey my voice indeed,
and keep my covenant, then ye shall be a peculiar
treasure unto me above all people: for all the earth
is mine:
Exodus 19:5

Scotty was pleased with how his circumstances were going. He did not need any bossy leader to tell him what to do, nor did he need a God who was so strict with all His rules and commandments. He hated how Brock and Margie were always quoting Scripture, reminding him of what Jesus said in the Sermon on the Mount, and about loving each other and doing what was right. He did not need to follow anyone. He knew when Bruno took one look at his map and found his treasure, why, he would kick McAllister down from his smug seat of first mate and promote Scotty to be his right hand man! Scotty grinned up at Bruno as they approached his hiding spot in the woods near the orchard. He pointed to the 'X' made by the two trees where he had hidden the map. "See? 'X' marks the spot. It's right under there."

McAllister bent down and moved the rock away, and pulled up the little leather pouch. He handed it to Bruno and then looked at Scotty with a questioning look.

Unnerved by the man's stare, Scotty turned away. He had no idea why McAllister would be looking at him that way. It was as if he were trying to send an unspoken message to him, like "Run while you can." Why should he run? Bruno was about to discover the best thing there was on earth and he was not about to run away and hide! This was his chance for fame and fortune!

After examining the map for a few minutes, Bruno and his men hiked back inside the castle. He kept a close eye on Scotty, though he should not have worried about him wandering off. Scotty was not going to miss this for the world!

They climbed up to the third floor and entered a room that had once been an old chapel. The room contained a few rows of rotted wooden seats that faced a large, hand carved pulpit with a cross on it. Bruno examined each wall, pushing and shoving as hard as he could, but he could not find a secret door anywhere. He checked the map again, trying to pinpoint the exact spot where the door was located. Looking around the room, he spotted the old pulpit at the front of the room. He gave it a push and it moved to the side, revealing a hole underneath. He let out an excited shout. "Would you look at that? To think they used the old pulpit to hide their secret door! What a brilliant idea!"

The gaping hole looked like a giant mouth waiting to swallow them all up, but that did not stop Bruno from going inside. He touched the walls activating the glowing rocks. Thick cobwebs hung down from the floor to the ceiling, and the passageway smelled musty and dank.

Scotty felt a little afraid of going inside. What if there was a giant spider waiting around the corner wanting a fat, juicy boy for dinner? After all, how many years had it been since somebody had gone into the tunnel? Bruno did not hesitate though and began making his way down the stairs, not caring about the dense sticky cobwebs.

From behind, Scotty felt a gentle shove by McAllister, and he stepped forward, relieved to see that the big man had cleared most of the webs away. They followed the stairs down, deep into the belly of the castle, and after a little way the stairs turned into a tunnel underground leading into the mountainside. Twisting and turning, the path continued on, with little forks veering off into every direction. Bruno never said a word, only pausing now and then to check the map he held in his hands. He finally reached his destination and gave a cry of anticipation.

The room was large, with old barrels scattered across the floor. Empty crates were stacked high in each corner of the room and old, tattered sheets hung, as if they had once been used as dividers many years before.

At the back of the room, a giant hole caught all of their attention. In disbelief, Bruno approached the hole and jumped inside. There were a few seconds of silence, and then a low grumbling began from below. The rumble became a roar of anger as Bruno burst out of the hole and leaped toward Scotty.

"Where is it? You promised me no tricks! Where did you hide it?" He grabbed Scotty's shoulders and shook him, just as he had done to Brock hours before.

McAllister stepped forward and grabbed Bruno's hands, risking his own neck to protect the boy. When Bruno did not stop, McAllister shoved Bruno backwards and sent him sprawling into the hole. Scotty almost followed him in, but McAllister's firm hands managed to catch him before he went over the side.

Bruno let out a shriek of pain, and immediately the other sailors rushed forward to assist him. They pulled Bruno out and helped him gain his footing. Holding his right arm,

Bruno glared at McAllister and Scotty, "You two are going to regret you ever defied me!" He growled. "Pete and Monty, you take these two and lock them up in the hold of the ship. Do not let them get away or it will mean your life. I have to do some business with that Brock kid. He must know where the treasure is hidden."

Still favoring his arm, Bruno made his way back out of the tunnels, knowing his sailors would take care of McAllister and Scotty. His arm appeared to be broken, but the anger and disappointment he felt kept him moving forward. He had spent years looking for his grandfather's treasure. He wondered why his father had never searched for the island, but he was glad he was the one who had found the castle. However, if he returned without anything to show for his searching, after coming this close to finding the treasure, he would be a laughing stock to his whole family. They had never believed there was any treasure in the first place, and he wanted to show them they were wrong!

* * * * * * * * *

Meanwhile, back inside the room where the orphans sat, Nellie had approached Margie and sat down beside her. Looking up into her face, she earnestly asked Margie to explain about what Jesus had done on the cross. Margie happily began telling her about John 3:16, how God had so loved the world that He gave His only begotten Son, that whosoever would believe in Him should not perish but have everlasting life.

"You see, Nellie, all men have sinned and come short of the glory of God. Because the first man Adam sinned in the garden, sin and death entered the world, and a gap formed between God and man. Men sacrificed spotless lambs for years and years to wash away their sins, but those lambs never could wash away their sin. Then one day, God sent an angel to a virgin girl name Mary. He told her she was going to have a son, and He would be the Son of God. She had a baby boy she named Jesus, and when He grew up He became the final sacrifice for humanity. He was the perfect, spotless Lamb needed to bridge that gap that sin had formed between God and man. When the evil men put Him up on the cross, He kept silent and even forgave those who killed Him. He knew His sacrifice and death was necessary, and wanted to obey His Father because He loved us so much." Margie paused, and Brock stepped in and continued where she left off.

"The best part about it is the fact that after three days, Jesus rose from the dead. Our God is not a dead God, but One Who is alive and hears every prayer we pray to Him. Our sins, forgiven that day, can be washed away by calling on the name of Jesus. Believe on the Lord, acknowledge that we are sinners, repent and confess our sins, and ask Him to come live in our hearts. He will save us and grant us eternal life with Him in Heaven."

"And what happens if we don't do that?" Kato asked.

Brock answered, "The ones who refuse to call on the name of the Lord will go to Hell, which is a place of torment and fire. It is a horrible place with pain, darkness, and weeping."

Kato looked at Bryan and saw by the tears in his eyes that Bryan had been deeply affected by Margie and Brock's words. "I want to ask Jesus into my heart. I have never known the peace you seem to have, and I want it. Can I do it right now?"

"Can I too?" Nellie eagerly leaned forward, putting her hand on Margie's arm.

"Oh, yes, of course you can!"

They all bowed their heads and prayed, and three new souls found Christ that very hour.

When the final amen's were said, Margie reached out and hugged her new sister in the Lord. "Welcome to God's family!" she said, wiping away her tears.

To her surprise, Nellie sat back and began pulling up the sleeve of her dress.

"I have to show you something," she said excitedly.

All the children watched curiously, as Nellie pulled up the long sleeve of her dress and held out her arm. There, at the top, close to her shoulder, was a bright red birthmark in the shape of a cross. Nellie's voice was hoarse when she spoke. "And to think this spot caused me so much grief – from the day I was born, my people have looked down upon me because they thought I had the mark of the devil. You just taught me that the cross is the only thing that can save us from our sins and bring us back to God. After all these years, I realize it was God Who had marked me from the moment I was born!"

"Oh, Nellie, He knew you even before you were born," Margie cried, hugging Nellie again. "I'm sorry you've had to struggle so much all these years. I should warn you though; just because you are a Christian now does not mean you won't ever have any trials. Life may not get any easier, but we do have the Lord's promise to never leave us or forsake us. He will give us strength to deal with what comes our way. He keeps us in the palm of His hand forever. He loves you so, dear child."

A thought suddenly occurred to Bryan. "Nettle, your mother is the daughter of Pearlie, who was the daughter of Queen Lily, which makes you the great granddaughter of the queen. You are a princess!"

Nellie's eyes shone as she thought about her Uncle's comment, then added, "I may be the great granddaughter of a queen, but now I am the daughter of a King!"

They all laughed happily at her comment, excited for Nellie and her prospect of having a bright future.

Just then, the door burst open, and Bruno barged into the room favoring his right arm. His booming voice shook the room, causing the littlest children to whimper and hide their heads in Margie and Tina's laps. "You!" he shouted, pointing at Brock. "Get up and come with me!" he commanded.

Puzzled, Brock stood up and walked over to Bruno. "Grab him men, and don't let him get away!" Two men roughly grabbed hold of Brock's arms and started pulling him out the door.

"Where are you taking him?" Margie shouted, uncomfortable with what was happening. She watched as they dragged Brock out the door and down the hall. Not wanting to be left behind, she hurried through the door after the men. She glanced around for Scotty briefly wondering where he could be.

Bryan slowly stood up on wobbly legs, grabbing the wall for support. "We must follow them, Kato. Brock knows nothing except for what we told him. We need to go and help him."

Kato agreed and stood up, grabbing a hold of Bryan's arm to help steady him. Together they walked down the hall, with Mark on the other side of Bryan. They went through the door just in time to see Bruno's men tying Brock's arms behind the big tree in the middle of the courtyard.

CHAPTER TWENTY-ONE

Great Trouble

Better *is* little with the fear of the LORD than great
treasure and trouble therewith.
Proverbs 15:16

High up on the lookout cliff, Matthew had been watching
the events unfold before his eyes. Earlier, his pride
had begun to shatter as he had watched two men haul a
kicking, screaming little boy down the trail that led to the
beach. A third man had followed close behind led by a rope
tied around his wrists. Now, he could clearly see into the
courtyard of the fortress, where the bandits were gathering
around the tree. It was obvious that the group of bandits was
not treating the children as friends. Something was not right
down there. With this revelation, he realized that his first
instincts about the children being friends with the Jellyfish
had all been wrong.

He snuck down the cliff and peered into the courtyard,
hoping to get a closer look at what was going on. He saw the
young man tied up to a tree. His face was pointed upwards
toward the sky, his eyes closed. Bryan and Kato were standing

nearby pleading for the boy's life. Matthew knew he had to act fast. He practically flew up to his lookout point and blew his shell in quick rapid gusts sounding the village alarm.

Hearing the quick bursts, the villagers all stopped what they were doing and paused, wondering at the sound. They hardly had ever heard that particular alarm, except for the time when it was taught to them, and it took a minute to dawn on them what the meaning was.

It was Buttercup, Bryan's wife, who took action. "Quick, everyone, there is trouble down at the fortress! We must go and help!"

The villagers rallied together as quickly as they could and began to make their way down the path that led to the castle.

Everyone in the courtyard stopped when the shrill blasts of the shell rang through the air. Bryan and Kato exchanged looks and knew that help was coming. Of course, Matthew had seen it all from his perch up on the mountain; nothing ever seemed to get passed him! They just hoped he would not be too late! Bryan knew he had to do all he could to keep Bruno distracted.

"Brock knows nothing of the treasure, but I can tell you where it is if you will spare the boy's life!"

"You know where the treasure is? How do I know you won't trick me like that brat did?"

"I can assure you this is no trick. Mordecai took the treasure out of the caves and buried it elsewhere. I can lead you to it if you will untie Brock."

A commotion outside the castle gate made everyone look up. A group of people was tramping over the drawbridge, with sticks, stones and strange looking weapons.

"What in the world?" Bruno muttered. "Will this foolishness never end?"

Matthew was in the lead, with Pearlie right behind him. Sadie and Raul were behind them. When Nellie saw her mother and father, she rushed forward and fell into her mother's arms.

"I'm sorry for running away, Momma, but I had to do what I did. Please forgive me!"

Sadie pulled her daughter close and gave her a great big hug. "Hush now, my child. It will be all right. Everything will be all right." She closed her eyes in relief as she patted her daughter's hair.

Matthew marched up to Bruno and stood before him. "I am Matthew, leader of King Farrell's tribe. Can we work out a deal to let the boy go?"

Bruno smirked and cocked his head to the side. "I think we already have a deal, if Bryan is telling the truth. He has agreed to show me where the treasure is if I will untie the boy. Can I trust him?"

"Of course you can. Moreover, he won't be the only one who will take you there. My people and I will show you the way."

Bruno motioned to the two sailors standing next to Brock, and they quickly untied him from the tree.

Margie rushed over to him and gave him a quick hug. "Oh Brock, I never stopped praying for your safety. The Lord is so good to us," she said.

Brock looked at her tenderly and commented, "Margie, even if they had killed me the Lord would still be good to us."

Margie blinked in surprise as his words made an impact on her. Then she nodded and whispered, "Yes, He would be, but I am so glad He chose to keep you around longer."

It was a long line of people that walked to the village, following Matthew and Pearlie, with Bruno and his men right behind them.

Bryan decided to stay at the castle because he still did not have the strength to walk the distance to his home. Buttercup remained with him, happy to be reunited with her husband.

Their three children, Summer, Wheaton, and baby Tomas, gathered close to their father and listened as he told them all that had transpired in the last few days.

Best of all, he told them about his newfound faith, and how such a wonderful peace had come over him since he had received the Lord as his Savior.

Buttercup could see it in his eyes and marveled at the change in him. He was no longer the beaten down, depressed husband she had always known. She could not wait to hear more so she could learn of this peace too.

* * * * * * * * *

Matthew stood in front of a little hut and announced, "This is it. You will find the treasure inside this hut."

"In there?" Bruno looked skeptical. "Is this someone's home?"

"Nobody lives in it. It is our main meetinghouse and we hardly ever use it. Go ahead and start digging. It should not be more then five feet below ground."

With four strong men digging, it did not take long for them to strike the metal box. They pulled up a large, rusty trunk and set it on the ground in front of everyone. Bruno rubbed his hands together as he knelt down in front of the box. The latch simply fell off in his hand from all the years of sitting in the ground. Bruno opened the box, which revealed thousands of gold pieces. His eyes glittered in excitement as he picked up a handful and let them fall through his fingers. "I am a rich man," he uttered happily. "I am the richest man in the whole world!"

Closing the cover of the box, Bruno stood up and barked some orders to his men. With two men each taking a side, they picked it up and began their descent down the mountain to the beach. Bruno glanced back at Brock and sneered, "Goodbye, preacher boy. Maybe someday your missionary will find you again. If not, then I expect your rotting carcasses will still be here if I should ever come looking for more gold, not that there is any more now that I own it all. Ha ha!" With that, Bruno turned and followed after his group of rough sailors.

"Are they gone?" a woman asked from the back of the crowd. "You don't think they'll come back, do you?" Fear was in her voice at the thought of what the bandits were capable of doing.

"No, I think their greed has been satisfied for the time being. They should not be back for a long time. He got what he came for, but whether it will bring him fame and fortune, who knows? It might just bring him death too. Riches never did anything for anybody." Matthew stopped talking and looked sadly after the men who had so quickly disappeared with the loot. It was not that he would miss the money, because they never had any need for it. What bothered him was the fact that after all these years, all their work of hiding and guarding the treasure was over. Now what would they do to occupy their time on this lonely island?

Suddenly Margie gave a little gasp of dismay. "Where's Scotty?"

CHAPTER TWENTY-TWO

Changes for Scotty

S cotty sat quietly in the hold of the ship, with his back against one of the walls. It was pitch black, and he had no idea where he was or what lay beyond the area where he sat. McAllister had been with him for a little while, but they had hardly spoken to each other, unsure of what to say. Scotty did not know how long they sat there, but it felt like hours.

McAllister finally broke the silence after they had heard banging and loud laughing above their heads. "Sounds like they found what they were looking for," he commented.

"You mean they found the treasure?" Scotty asked, leaning as far forward as his chains would allow. "That means we'll go free!"

"Don't be too sure of that, lad. Bruno is a tough master, and he won't let you go that easy. You failed him the first time, and that will be the last time I ever fail him. He will never give me another chance. He never gives anyone another chance. We're done for."

Just at that moment, the hatch opened and long legs descended the ladder. The sailor came down with a lantern in his hand and walked over to McAllister.

"The Captain wants to see you up on deck," he said as he unlocked McAllister's chains. "No funny business or you will be food for the sharks," he said gruffly as he shoved McAllister up the ladder in front of him. Turning around for a second, he glanced back at Scotty. "Don't go away kid, he'll be back!" A low, deep gurgle of a laugh ascended from his broad stomach and the sound echoed in the hold.

"Like I can go anywhere," Scotty mumbled to himself. "This is the worse thing that could happen to me. I had no idea my turning against the others would end up like this. I would rather be listening to Brock order me around then be locked up in chains in the pitch black. I hate the dark!"

Scotty had always tried to look and act braver then his nine years, but the despair that settled down on him was too much for his little mind to comprehend. The darkness, the sounds of the water splashing behind the wall he was leaning on, and the cold, metal feeling of the chains around his wrists were too much. He could not keep back the tears that threatened to spill from his eyelids.

Memories of his father walking away flashed before his eyes and the sobs grew louder. He could not wipe the large droplets away with his hands tied, so he turned and rubbed his eyes on his ragged shoulder sleeves. He felt so low and depressed that he did not know what to do. Suddenly, Margie's voice floated into his head, "You can always try praying, Scotty. The Lord can be your Father if you ask Him into your heart. He loves the fatherless. When you ask Him into your heart, He promises to take care of you forever. The next time you get into trouble, remember to call on His Name."

A scene from a little over a year ago, replayed in his mind: he had gotten in trouble with Mrs. Talley for taking some bread from the orphanage kitchen. She had punished him by taking away his supper. He had spent the evening on his bed, with his face to the wall, mad at how unfair the world was.

Margie had crept into the room after dinner and handed him a piece of meat and an apple. As he ate, she encouraged him with her words, but he never thought much about it at the time. Now that he was in trouble though, her words kept playing repeatedly in his head. "The next time you are in trouble, remember to call on His Name."

He decided that he would try it. Nobody was around to laugh or make fun of him, so he bowed his head and closed his eyes.

"Dear Jesus, I'm sorry for rejecting you all these years and causing a lot of trouble. I'm sorry for what I have done, and I ask that You will forgive me and come help me out of this mess. I promise I will be good if You just get me out of here and help me make things right. Get me back to Margie and Brock so I can tell them I am sorry for what I said and how I acted. Please come live in my heart and be the Father that I have been missing all these years. In Jesus' Name, Amen."

He opened his eyes, almost expecting to see a bright light or something, but the darkness still surrounded him. As he sat, a funny thing began to happen inside of him: the despair and anger began to melt away, and in its place peace came to rule and reign inside his heart. An unspeakable joy filled his whole being, and he knew without a doubt that no matter what happened he was the Lord's child now. God would take care of him!

* * * * * * * * *

A loud bump made Scotty jump. He had fallen asleep against the side of the wall and his neck ached from the angle he had slept in. He sat up and glanced towards the ladder. McAllister was coming down the ladder, along with two sailors who were helping him. They led him to his spot near Scotty and chained him up again. Without a word, they took the lantern and went back up, closing the hatch behind them. A moan escaped from the man's lips, and Scotty sat up.

"Are you okay?" he asked McAllister.

"If you had fifteen lashes on your back, would you be okay? I can't even lean back against the wall to rest!"

Another moan drifted over to Scotty, and he felt a twinge of regret in his stomach. That poor man – why, he had been beaten because of Scotty and his rash reactions! Scotty wanted to do something for him, but did not know what or how.

"Is there something I can do for you?"

"I have a key in my pocket. Can you reach it somehow?"

"My hands are tied behind my back, but I could try and use my feet."

He stretched out his leg as far as he could and felt McAllister's leg.

"It's in my left side pocket. I will turn as best I can for you to get the key out."

Scotty tried and tried to pull the key out, but the pocket was too tight for his foot to slip into.

"I can't do it," he said. "It's too tight. I'm sorry."

"Don't worry. Let's rest for a few minutes and try again. I am not about to let Bruno do any more to me. I swiped that key from his quarters when he was briefing me about how improper my actions were. He may be captain, but I am not going to follow his orders anymore. He's just downright evil inside!"

It was silent again and Scotty figured the man was resting. Soon, McAllister began talking again and asked Scotty how old he was.

"I'm nine years old."

"I once had a son; he would be about your age too."

"What happened to him?" Scotty asked, a curious feeling starting to spread over him.

"His mother died when he was only three years old. I could not take care of him and give him a good home. I left the boy at an orphanage when he was very young. He did not want me to leave, but I turned my back on him and abandoned him. I could not look back or else my heart would have broken." A sob escaped the man's lips as he continued, "I would give anything to go back and see him again, if I knew he would forgive me for what I did."

Scotty could barely believe his ears – could this man be his long-lost father? He decided to test his theory out.

"Maybe your son *would* forgive you if he knew you were really sorry."

"What I did was wrong. I am sure he hates me, if he even thinks of me."

"He used to hate you for leaving," Scotty commented, "But something happened to change him."

A metal chain clanged as McAllister moved to sit up. "What? What are you saying? How would you know?" There was a frightened tone in the man's voice. Funny how a big, strong sailor man could sound frightened!

"My name is Scott McAllister. My mother was Meghan McAllister. She died of disease when I was three years old. Shortly after, my father left me at an orphanage."

His first real memory played over in his mind again, with the same cutting pain in the pit of his stomach. He remembered crying for his mother and his father shushing him, telling him that she would never be coming back. Scotty had not understood all the changes happening in his young life, so he clung to his father, the only bit of security left to the three year old. Then a few days later his father had taken him to a large house and handed him over to Mrs. Talley. Scotty remembered crying and holding his chubby arms out to his father. His father had turned around without a word and fled out the door, unable to look back. That had been his last memory of his father.

Suddenly, a new image played in his mind – a strong man standing up for him as another man tried to hurt him. The old memory began to fade in his mind as the fresh one took its place. His father loved his son and wanted him to forgive him!

McAllister was silent, and Scotty wondered if he was okay. "McAllister? Are you all right?"

He could hear the sound of quiet sobbing, and Scotty knew he had to get out of his chains.

"I'm going to get that key," he stated and began anew, trying to dig the key out of the pocket with his toes. It took several tries, but finally it clinked on the wooden floor. Scotty dragged it closer with his foot. Bending over sideways, as far as the chains would allow him, he managed to grab the key with his fingers. His back ached from stretching so far, but he ignored the pain. With the key behind him, he felt around for the lock and popped the key in. With one click, his hands were free!

Rushing forward, Scotty felt around for McAllister's chains and quickly unlocked them. The key fell to the floor unnoticed as the two grabbed each other in a tight hug, though McAllister moaned at Scotty's touch on his back.

Scotty pulled his arms away feeling horrible for causing his father more pain. "I'm sorry for getting you into this mess! Will you forgive me?"

"I should be the one asking you to forgive me," McAllister sighed, tucking Scotty close to his legs, away from his back, but still wanting to be close to him. "But if it wasn't for you then we would never have found each other!"

"Yes," agreed Scotty. "Like the Bible says, all things do work for good to them that love God and are called according to His purpose."

"You know the Bible?" McAllister asked, shocked.

"Yes, I do, and now I have a changed heart!" Scotty told him.

"I don't understand. How did you get a new heart?" McAllister asked him.

Scotty replied, "I finally found my Heavenly Father down here while you were up with Bruno. I asked Him to come into my heart today and now I am born again. Jesus granted me forgiveness for all I have done, and all that was done to me. If I had found out who you were before today, I would have never spoken to you. Jesus forgave me for my sins, and now I can forgive you for what you did. I am not mad anymore."

"I'm sure a nine year old could not have committed too many sins. I'm the one that needs forgiveness. The truth is that I did not really want to leave you, Scott. I was heart-broken about your mother, and I knew nothing about caring for a child. I could not give you the proper clothing, food, or education you needed. I decided I would leave you in better hands and maybe someday come back and get you, but the look on your face when I left was unbearable. I did not think you would ever forgive me. I went to the pier to end my life; I was going to jump into the sea, but Bruno found me and offered me a job to join his crew. He was on a mission to find the lost treasure of his grandfather Jared Bones. We have been looking for that treasure for six years."

Scotty was dumbstruck at the possibility of having his father back after all these years. It was as if they had come full circle. With the guidance of the Lord's hands, all the pain and anguish from the last seven years were erased. They had an opportunity to start over again - if they ever got out of this alive!

The hatch swung open again and the same long legs from before descended the ladder.

"Not again," moaned McAllister.

Scotty put his hand protectively over his father's knee. As an after thought, he felt around for the key and quickly shoved it behind a sack near his back. He did not want anyone to find it just in case it was needed again.

Monty, one of the men Bruno had placed as a guard over the two, stood looking down at them with the light of the lantern.

"How did you two get loose?" he asked, then shrugged. "No matter; you must come with me. The Captain wants to see you both."

Scotty helped McAllister up, and together they climbed the ladder. After sitting in the dark for so long, the bright sunlight hurt their eyes. They waited outside the door of Captain Bruno's quarters with Monty right beside them. Scotty looked around at his surroundings and realized the ship was moving! He wondered how long they had been sailing, and how far they were from the island. He hoped he could get back soon.

The door of the Captain's quarters opened, and Bruno stepped out. He held a paper in his hand, and he was grinning from ear to ear. Scotty noticed a second person in the cabin, who followed Bruno out onto the deck.

"Mr. Carver!"

The man turned and looked at Scotty with such a relieved look of joy. His eyes brimmed over with tears as he ran forward and grasped little Scotty in his strong arms!

"Scotty! Oh, how I've longed to see your face again!"

Scotty pressed his face against Mr. Carver's rough overcoat and sobbed with joy. He could hardly believe what God had done for him in just a few short hours, and he had never felt so good! Suddenly remembering his father, he pulled back and grabbed his father's hand.

"Mr. Carver," he sniffed and brushed away a tear, "I would like to introduce you to John McAllister, my father!"

It was Bruno's turn to look aghast at Scotty's words.

"Father?" he said in disbelief. "What has been happening down in the hold for the last two days?"

"Two days?" Scotty said. "We have been down there that long?"

"Joy covers many things such as hunger and pain," remarked Mr. Carver. "Oh, Scotty, I'm so happy for you." Turning to McAllister he said, "And it's my pleasure to meet you, Mr. McAllister."

Scotty tugged on Mr. Carver's arm again. "And that isn't all." His eyes sparkled with his other news, "I also met my heavenly Father today too."

Again, tears brimmed over as Mr. Carver rejoiced with Scotty in his conversion. "I can already tell that you have changed, Scotty. You are not the same boy I knew over a month ago."

Not comfortable with the talk of religion, Bruno stepped forward. "Let's get down to business, Preacher Man. You agreed to take these two as servants on your ship. You promised to take them in exchange for water and food. Now that the exchange is done you are free to take them away."

They shook hands and Mr. Carver began to make his way to the lifeboat. It was then that Scotty noticed the other ship sailing parallel to the *Jellyfish*. The words on the side said, *Haven*.

Scotty and Mr. Carver helped McAllister over the side and into the boat. Without another word to Bruno or his men, Scotty got in and sat down next to his father. Mr. Carver looked back at Bruno as his own sailors lowered the boat down to the water.

"I will be praying for you, Bruno. Even a tough man like you needs salvation and forgiveness of sins." He gave a slight wave as the sailors rowed them over to the *Haven*.

Scotty could barely contain his excitement. "So you survived the fire! What happened to you? Where have you been all this time?"

Mr. Carver looked grim. "We have been looking for you for the last three weeks. After we put out the fire, we went to retrieve you from the lifeboat and discovered it gone. Our hearts sank at the thought of you drifting out there for days. I prayed for your safety and protection every moment while we searched for you. You were nowhere to be found. We had to get new supplies and repair the damage done by the fire, so we sailed to the nearest harbor. We were there for a week and then we set back out to sea after we repaired the boat, and we have been searching ever since that day. It was only by the grace of God that we came upon Captain Bruno's ship and were able to ask him if he had any knowledge of islands around this area. He showed me the map and pointed out the Island of Farrell. It was so small and hidden, and unclaimed by any country, that no maps have recorded it. He had some sort of a treasure map, which he claimed was the only one that listed the island. Then he asked if he could trade some prisoners for food. Without even knowing who the prisoners were, I felt the Lord telling me to say yes. I am so glad I followed the Lord's guidance!"

Safely aboard the *Haven,* Scotty helped his father to a bunk and washed the stripes on his back. McAllister felt much better afterwards and drifted off to sleep. Scotty fell down on his knees beside his father's bed and thanked the Lord for His mercy and for not giving up on him.

CHAPTER TWENTY-THREE

The Providence of God

Three long days passed with no word from Scotty. The orphans had no idea what had become of him and prayed continually for his safety. The villagers gladly took in the children and they all soon became friends, happy that there was no longer a misunderstanding of who they were. The villagers were very happy to meet some new people, and they also let the children help them work in the gardens and with the livestock.

Bryan and his family returned from the fortress during that time and were welcomed back home with open arms. Kato also recovered from his trying experience, and Matthew apologized to them for the harsh judgment he had wreaked on them.

"I only meant well for the villagers," he explained. "I was trying to protect everyone."

"I understand," said Bryan, "And I forgive you. God has helped me to overcome many things in the last couple of days, and He has given me a new heart."

It was Sunday morning, and all the villagers gathered around for Brock's Sunday service. He led them all in a hymn; singing was something new to them, as they had never done it before. Because they expressed a desire to learn the song, Brock sang it many times until most of the people had learned the verses. Afterwards, he preached a sermon on their need for salvation in their lives and many of the villagers were saved that morning.

After the service was over, they all gathered around and enjoyed a lunch of lamb, fruit, and bread, which the villagers made from the wheat they grew in a nearby field. It was while they were eating that the shrill blast of the shell echoed through the village.

Startled, Matthew looked up. Who could be blowing the horn? What danger was there now?

Matthew quickly rallied the men together and hurried to the lookout cliff.

Raul stood on the edge, pointing down at the castle. "There are some men at the fortress!" he announced.

Together, Matthew led his men down the path to the castle drawbridge. He carefully peered around the corner and looked into the courtyard. He saw a boy standing in front of some men and he was waving his arms frantically shouting, "They just have to be here! Where could they have gone?"

Bryan recognized Scotty and touched Matthew's arm. "That is the lost boy the children have been talking about. He was the one who turned against them."

Hearing some scuffling outside the gate, Mr. Carver looked towards the bridge. He noticed all the men standing outside and waved them in. "Come on in, gentlemen! You're welcome to come and talk to us!"

Scotty turned and saw Bryan and Kato. He ran over to them. "Where is everyone? Are they okay?"

Bryan nodded. "Yes, they are fine, Scotty. They are at the village. They have been worried sick about you."

Scotty frowned. "They have been worried sick about me? Why, that's not like Margie and Brock at all!"

"Why do you say that?"

"Because usually they just take it to the Lord and cast all their cares on Him."

Bryan smiled at the boy's words. "They are still human, Scotty. We don't always do what is right all the time."

Scotty shrugged and grabbed his father's hand. "Let's go find them! I can't wait to see their faces when they hear my news *and* see Mr. Carver!"

* * * * * * * * *

It was not long before Matthew led the group into the village, and the first thing Scotty saw was his group of friends gathered in a circle, looking apprehensive. He knew they were worried about who these strangers were. He saw Brock stand up and shade his eyes, trying to see against the glare of the sun.

Scotty waved and ran forward. "Brock!" he called.

Brock stepped forward. "Scotty, is that you?"

"Yes! I am back!" he called. "And you will never guess who found me!"

Margie looked past Brock and saw the tall man first. A shout of joy flew from her lips, and she darted forward unable to contain herself. "Mr. Carver! Mr. Carver! Oh, praise the Lord! It's Mr. Carver! He's alive!"

When the realization dawned on all the children that Mr. Carver was truly there, they all ran forward and leaped upon him, hugging him, until he disappeared behind all the bodies of his dear orphans.

Scotty stood back smiling, but a little hurt that nobody had hugged him in joy too.

Teddy was the first to notice Scotty standing alone. He ran over and gave him a great big bear hug. "Welcome home, Scotty. We missed you so much!"

Margie heard Teddy's comment and hurried over too. Suddenly, the huge pile around Mr. Carver moved like a mighty wave until they buried Scotty. The villagers laughed and cried as they witness the love and tenderness displayed by all the orphans for their fellow believers. It was a moment nobody would ever forget.

Brock looked a little startled to see McAllister standing off to the side. "What is he doing here?" Brock asked Mr. Carver. "Does that mean Bruno is around somewhere too?"

Mr. Carver shook his head. "No, do not fear children. Bruno made me promise to never return my two new servants."

"Servants?" Margie asked.

"Yes. It is a long story, which I will explain later, but for now, I think I will let Scotty tell you about McAllister."

Everyone turned towards Scotty, eager to hear what he had to say.

Scotty cleared his throat, obviously nervous about being the center of attention. "Well, it is a long story, and like Mr. Carver said, we will explain more of it later. But first, I need to make an apology, especially to you, Brock and Margie, about how wicked I have been. I am sorry for being so rebellious and stubborn. The Lord convicted me of my sinful heart when I was a prisoner in Bruno's ship. It was there that I met the Lord and He became my Savior."

Cheers of joy resounded from everyone and Margie ran forward to embrace Scotty again. "All is forgiven, Scotty. Welcome to the family!"

Brock stepped forward and mussed Scotty's hair. "No hard feelings, Scotty. Sometimes God uses the hard times to get our attention." He smiled down at Scotty and then glanced at Margie. Both had tears in their eyes.

"That's not all," Scotty continued. "I also met my real father down in the hold too. Everybody, I want you to meet my father, John McAllister."

The group was shocked into silence. Scotty's father was alive?

Margie looked closely at McAllister. It had been about six years since she had seen his face, which looked much older now, but the red hair was as bright as she had ever remembered it. Both McAllister and Scotty had the same freckles on their noses — there was no doubt that they were related! She smiled warmly and said, "What wonderful news! Mr. McAllister, we are very pleased to meet you. We're so happy you and Scotty found each other. Welcome to our group!"

Brock looked around for Mr. Carver and noticed he was deeply absorbed in his Bible and seemed oblivious to what was going on around him. Brock walked over to him and touched his arm. "Mr. Carver?"

Mr. Carver glanced up and smiled. "Children, I wanted to share with you something the Lord impressed upon my heart. What we have seen here today is God's providence at work. It was certainly the will of God for the events of the last month to take place. Although Scotty was disobedient and rebellious, the consequences of his sin drew him to the Savior and God's grace allowed him to be reunited with his father. I am reminded of a verse in Isaiah fifty-five, verse eight. It says, 'For my thoughts are not your thoughts, neither are your ways my ways, saith the LORD. For as the heavens are higher than the earth, so are my ways higher than your ways, and my thoughts than your thoughts.' It's hard to imagine that God would use a fire, castle, treasure, *and* a crew of bandits to bring about His perfect will. It makes me very excited to think about what the Lord has in store for our future. Let's all kneel down and take the time to thank our Lord for all He has done for us and will continue to do."

They knelt down and each took a turn praising and thanking God for His love and mercy. The villagers watched in amazement at the love that was displayed. They thought it fitting to host a feast in honor of their new guests. Matthew waited for the children to finish, and then approached Mr. Carver with his invitation, who gladly accepted.

Throughout the afternoon and evening, Mr. Carver listened to the adventures the children told about their time spent on the island, and in turn, he answered their questions about what had happened to the ship after the fire. When all the stories were told and the bellies were filled, Mr. Carver did what he had always done: with all the villagers, orphans, and crew members of the *Haven* before him, Mr. Carver once again took out his Bible and gave a short devotional they could meditate on as they fell asleep. A sense of peace settled over the orphans, one they had not felt since they had last seen Mr. Carver. They had a renewed sense of hope that whether they stayed on the island or continued their journey, God would always be watching over them.